TINY TALES OF NASRUDDIN

Tiny Tales of Nasruddin

A Book of Two Hundred 100-Word Stories

Laura Gibbs

CONTENTS

ABOUT THIS BOOK

Stories of Nasruddin date back to 13th-century Turkey. Legend tells us Nasruddin was born in Sivrihisar in central Anatolia, and a tomb in Akshehir bears his name. Nasruddin's stories spread throughout the Middle East, South Asia, and Central Asia, and UNESCO declared 1996-1997 "The International Year of Nasruddin." As you read these stories, you will see that Nasruddin is sometimes wise, sometimes foolish, and sometimes both at once. The 200 stories in this book are just a small fraction of the Nasruddin story tradition. To find out more about Nasruddin and to read more Nasruddin stories, visit:
Nasruddin.LauraGibbs.net

The paragraph you just read about Nasruddin is 100 words long, as is this paragraph, and that's also the length of each story in this book. The stories go fast, but you can slow down when you find one you like. Read it again. Let it sink in. Maybe even write your own version of the story, using your imagination to add more details. Meanwhile, if you don't like a story, don't get bogged down; just move on to the next one. There are more 100-word stories about Nasruddin, along with stories from other cultural traditions, at:
100Words.LauraGibbs.net

THE STORIES

1. NASRUDDIN GALLOPS THROUGH THE MARKET

The town square was crowded for market day.

Then, all of a sudden, Nasruddin came galloping through the square on his donkey. It looked like he was about to fall off, barely holding onto the reins with one hand while struggling to keep his turban on with the other.

Nobody had ever seen Nasruddin or his donkey move this fast!

"Hey there, Nasruddin!" yelled one of his friends as Nasruddin rode by. "Just where are you going in such a hurry?"

Nasruddin shouted a reply as the donkey galloped past. "I honestly don't know! You need to ask the donkey!"

2. NASRUDDIN SHARES THE DONKEY'S LOAD

Nasruddin had gone into the forest to chop wood.

At day's end, he bundled up the wood but, instead of putting the bundle on the donkey, he put the bundle on his own head. He then clambered up on the donkey and rode into town.

"Nasruddin!" shouted one of his friends. "Why are you carrying that bundle of wood there on your head? Doesn't it hurt?"

"It does hurt," Nasruddin admitted, "but I wanted to help share the load."

"I still don't understand," said Nasruddin's friend, looking puzzled.

"The donkey is carrying me," explained Nasruddin, "but I'm carrying the wood."

3. NASRUDDIN'S DONKEY IS MISSING

Nasruddin's donkey was lost, but Nasruddin appeared to be happy, not sad. Instead of looking for his donkey, he sat drinking coffee in the coffeehouse.

Everyone was puzzled about this, knowing how much Nasruddin loved his donkey, and his donkey had now been missing for several days.

"I don't understand why you look so happy," someone finally said to him. "How can you smile like that when your donkey is lost?"

"I'm smiling because I'm not on the donkey," explained Nasruddin, taking another sip of his coffee. "Just imagine: if I were on the donkey, I would be lost too!"

4. WHY NASRUDDIN RIDES BACKWARDS

Nasruddin was riding his donkey to the school while his pupils walked behind him. Nasruddin sat backwards, facing the children.

"You look funny riding backwards!" they said.

"If I faced forward, I'd have my back to you," Nasruddin explained, "which wouldn't be nice. If I faced forward and you walked in front, your backs would be towards me, which also wouldn't be nice. If you walked in front facing backwards to see me, you wouldn't see where you're going and you'd probably fall down. So, me riding backwards facing you, just like this," he concluded, "is really the best solution!"

5. NASRUDDIN, HIS SON, AND THE DONKEY

Nasruddin was going to town with his son. Nasruddin walked while his son rode their donkey.

Someone saw them and scoffed. "Lazy boy! Why must your father walk?"

So the son got off, and Nasruddin got on.

Farther down the road, someone else saw them and said, "Cruel father, making your son walk!"

So they both rode the donkey.

"Poor donkey, carrying two riders!" said the next person they met.

So then they both got off.

"Idiots!" laughed the next person. "At least one of you should ride the donkey!"

"Take note, my son," Nasruddin said. "There's no pleasing everyone."

6. BORROWING NASRUDDIN'S DONKEY

A neighbor asked to borrow Nasruddin's donkey.

Nasruddin did not want to loan him the donkey, but he also did not want to appear to be ungenerous. So, he made up an excuse.

"I'm sorry, but I must say no," said Nasruddin. "The donkey is not here right now; I loaned him to my brother-in-law, and he still hasn't returned the donkey."

Then, at that very moment, the donkey let out a loud bray from inside the stable.

Before his neighbor could say anything, Nasruddin gave him a hard look. "Who are you going to believe: me, or the donkey?"

7. NASRUDDIN'S DONKEY CROSSES THE STREAM

Nasruddin was returning home from the market, and his donkey was carrying bags of salt.

On the way, they had to cross a stream. The donkey slipped, and the salt dissolved in the water. When the donkey stood back up, he found his load was lighter, and he trotted happily home.

The next time they came from the market, the donkey was carrying bags of wool. He decided to stumble on purpose but, instead of dissolving, the wool absorbed the water and weighed even more than before.

"You can't expect to get lucky every time!" Nasruddin said to the donkey.

8. NASRUDDIN'S SAINTLY DONKEY

Nasruddin sat in the coffeehouse, praising his remarkable donkey.

"Your donkey is indeed remarkable," said one of Nasruddin's friends. "I've always thought your donkey had a very saintly disposition. He is much more saintly than you are."

This took Nasruddin by surprise. "What do you mean my donkey is 'more saintly' than I am?"

"I mean that if we gave your donkey a choice between a bucket of water and a bucket of wine, he would drink the water, not the wine."

"There's nothing saintly about that!" exclaimed Nasruddin. "That just shows the donkey is less intelligent than I am."

9. NASRUDDIN'S FLYING DONKEY

Nasruddin decided to teach his donkey how to fly.

"Look at the bird! Just do that!" Nasruddin would say. "It's going to be harder because you don't have wings, but I know you can do it."

Finally, the day had arrived. Nasruddin took his donkey up to a high cliff. "Fly, donkey, fly!" he said as he pushed his donkey off the cliff.

The donkey sailed through the air, but only briefly. He hit the ground and died.

Nasruddin blamed himself. "I got so excited about teaching him how to fly that I forgot to teach him how to land."

10. NASRUDDIN COUNTS THE DONKEYS

Nasruddin was taking the village's donkeys, laden with grain, to the mill. There was Nasruddin's donkey, plus nine more.

Halfway there, Nasruddin counted. Only nine!

Worried, he got down and went looking for the lost donkey.

When he came back, he counted again: ten donkeys.

"Praise God!" he said. "The missing donkey returned."

Nasruddin got back on his donkey and continued the journey.

Later, he counted again. Only nine!

He dismounted, went looking, came back, and counted. Ten donkeys!

"Well, I better walk. When I'm riding, that wayward donkey escapes."

Nasruddin was just forgetting to count the donkey underneath him!

11. NASRUDDIN REPORTS A STOLEN DONKEY

A thief had stolen Nasruddin's donkey, so Nasruddin went to the police station to report the crime, hoping that the police would find the donkey-thief and get his donkey back.

"I want to report a theft!" Nasruddin shouted. "Someone has stolen my donkey. I need your help!"

The police officer took out a piece of paper, ready to write down Nasruddin's account of the events.

"Tell me what happened," he said.

"How can I possibly do that?" Nasruddin exclaimed. "I wasn't there when it happened! If I'd been there, I would have stopped the thief before he took my donkey."

12. THE DONKEY AND THE POLICE-CHIEF

Nasruddin's donkey was missing. "Have you seen my donkey?" he asked everyone, but no one had seen the donkey.

Nasruddin was about to give up, when one of the village children said, "I know what happened to your donkey. My uncle says the new police chief is a real donkey. So he must be your donkey!"

"That's impossible, boy," Nasruddin replied. "My donkey is smart enough as donkeys go, but he's not capable of taking bribes, and he wouldn't know how to frame people for crimes they didn't commit. And that means he's not qualified to be chief of police!"

13. NASRUDDIN'S BRIBE

Nasruddin needed the judge's signature on some documents, which meant a bribe, and Nasruddin didn't like bribes.

So, Nasruddin got a pot, filled it with mud, and put honey on top to make it look like a pot full of honey. Nasruddin gave this to the judge, and the judge gave him the signed documents.

The next day, the judge's servant delivered a message. "The documents were in error! Return them to the judge."

"The documents are fine," Nasruddin replied. "If the judge has a problem of his own, he should take that up with his conscience, not with me."

14. THE JUDGE'S BRAND-NEW SHOES

One night Nasruddin found the judge lying drunk in a ditch. Chuckling, he took the judge's brand-new shoes. They were just the right size!

The next day the judge complained that robbers had ambushed him. "They stole my brand-new shoes!" he yelled.

Nasruddin then strolled into court wearing the judge's shoes.

"Where did you get those?" the judge demanded.

"I met a drunken man last night, and he insisted I take them," Nasruddin replied with a smile. "Do you know who he is? I'll gladly return them. He was, I'm afraid, very drunk."

The judge glared at Nasruddin in reply.

15. NASRUDDIN AND THE SLAP

A man slapped Nasruddin on the face, so Nasruddin took the man to court, accusing him of assault.

The judge ordered that the man must give Nasruddin a gold coin by way of damages.

"I will go home, get the coin, and be back within an hour," the man promised.

Nasruddin waited for an hour, and then another hour.

When three hours had passed and the man still had not returned, Nasruddin got up and slapped the judge.

"I'm going home, Your Honor," he explained, "so when that man finally shows up, feel free to take the coin as compensation."

16. NASRUDDIN AND THE GOAT

Nasruddin and his neighbor were quarreling.

"You stink worse than a goat!" his neighbor said, so Nasruddin took him to court for slander.

The judge said, "Bring in a goat for comparison."

They brought in a goat, and when the judge leaned down to sniff the goat, he fainted. That's how bad the goat smelled.

They revived the judge with smelling salts, and then the judge said, "Now bring in Nasruddin."

They brought in Nasruddin, and both the judge and the goat fainted. That's how bad Nasruddin smelled.

They had to throw both Nasruddin and the goat out of court.

17. NASRUDDIN AND THE SACKS OF WHEAT

Nasruddin was caught taking sacks of wheat from his neighbor's barn. Nasruddin had done this before, and this time the neighbor took him to court.

"What do you have to say for yourself?" asked the judge.

"I'm just a fool," Nasruddin admitted. "I get confused about whose barn is whose, which wheat is mine or theirs. I'm not sure how I ended up with my neighbor's wheat in my wagon."

"If you're so easily confused," said the judge, "why don't you sometimes put your wheat in other people's wagons?"

"I may be a fool," Nasruddin replied, "but I'm not stupid!"

18. NASRUDDIN VISITS THE PRISONERS

As an act of charity, Nasruddin went to the prison to talk with all the prisoners and console them.

When they spoke, each inmate told Nasruddin that they were imprisoned unjustly. "I'm innocent," they told him, one after another.

One inmate, however, did not protest. "I'm guilty of my crimes," he said, "and that's why I'm here in prison."

As soon as Nasruddin heard that, he went to see the warden.

"You have to free this prisoner immediately!" Nasruddin told the warden. "Otherwise, he's going to be a terrible influence on all the innocent men you have locked up here."

19. THE BEGGAR AND THE FOOD VENDOR

A beggar eating a crust of stale bread stood next to a shish-kebab vendor, inhaling deeply. The smell made even his stale bread taste good.

"You must pay for the smell!" shouted the vendor.

When the poor man couldn't pay, the vendor took him to court.

Nasruddin was the judge.

He listened to them both, and then he took some coins from his pocket, cupped his hands, and shook the coins.

"Do you hear that sound?" he asked the vendor.

"Yes," said the vendor, perplexed.

"The sound of the coins is payment for the smell of the meat. Case dismissed!"

20. BITING YOUR OWN EAR

A wife dragged her husband into Nasruddin's courtroom.

"He bit my ear!" she shouted.

"You bit your own ear!" the husband shouted back at her.

"Impossible!" the wife replied. "Nobody can bite their own ear."

Nasruddin called for a recess and went into his chambers. He tried to bite his own ear, but only succeeded in falling down and bruising his forehead.

Nasruddin returned to the courtroom. "Check the wife: does she have bruises on her forehead?"

There were no bruises.

"I therefore conclude the wife did not bite her own ear," said Nasruddin. "The husband is guilty as charged."

21. NASRUDDIN AND THE CASE OF THE COW

Nasruddin's neighbor came running up, shouting loudly. "There's been a terrible accident!" he said to Nasruddin.

"What happened?" asked Nasruddin, alarmed.

"Your ox got loose and gored my cow to death," the neighbor explained. "Someone will have to pay!"

"What do you mean?" replied Nasruddin. "Surely you can't hold me responsible for what my ox did to your cow."

"Oh," said the neighbor, "I apologize. I must have gotten my words mixed up! I meant to say that my ox got loose and gored your cow to death."

"Oh!" said Nasruddin. "That changes everything. Someone really will have to pay!"

22. PAYMENT IN KIND

Nasruddin's neighbor stormed into Nasruddin's house.

"I demand justice!" the neighbor shouted. "Just now your dog viciously attacked my wife and bit her on the foot. You're going to have to pay!"

"Don't worry," Nasruddin replied calmly. "We can easily arrange payment in kind."

"What do you mean?" asked the neighbor.

"For example, I could send my wife to your house, and your dog could bite her on the foot," Nasruddin explained. "There is also this option: your wife could come over here and she could bite my dog on the foot. I'll let you decide what would be best."

23. NASRUDDIN TAKES SIDES

Two men who were quarreling came to Nasruddin.

"Please help us, Nasruddin!" said the first man.

"We need you to judge between us!" said the second man.

The first man presented his case, and when he was done, Nasruddin exclaimed, "You're right!"

The second man shouted, "You haven't even listened to my side of the story!"

That man then presented his case and when he was done, Nasruddin exclaimed again, "You're right!"

Nasruddin's wife, who had listened to the whole thing, remarked, "They can't both be right."

Nasruddin looked at his wife and exclaimed with a smile, "You're right too!"

24. GOOD GOOSE, BAD GOOSE

Nasruddin had a bad-tempered goose that was always hissing and trying to bite him, so he took the goose to the market to sell.

As he handed the goose to the goose-broker, Nasruddin warned him, "This is a badly-behaved goose. Be careful!"

"Don't worry," the broker said. "I'll get you a good price."

The broker then began yelling, "Buy the best goose here! A fine goose! Good-natured goose! Buy the best goose here!"

Nasruddin snatched his goose back from the broker.

"I'm not selling this goose at any price!" he exclaimed. "I never knew what a good goose I had."

25. NASRUDDIN AND THE OCEAN

Nasruddin once took a long journey all the way to the ocean's edge. This was the first time he had seen the ocean. He was astounded by the water stretching to the horizon, and the rise and fall of the waves mesmerized him.

He then bent down to take a drink and immediately spat it out. "Disgusting!" he yelled. "Luckily, I've got some real water here with me."

He reached for his water-flask and poured some fresh water into the ocean.

"It's true that you look very impressive," he said, "but you need to learn what real water tastes like!"

26. NASRUDDIN AND THE MILKMAN

Nasruddin had gone to the milkman to get a gallon of cow's milk. He waited in line and then presented the milkman with the container he had brought with him.

"A gallon of cow's milk," he said to the milkman.

"I'm sorry, Nasruddin," the milkman replied, "but the container you've brought is much too small. There's no way a gallon of cow's milk will fit into that container."

Nasruddin stood there thinking.

"I know!" he said at last. "Instead of a gallon of cow's milk, give me a gallon of goat's milk. Goat's milk will be just the right size!"

27. NASRUDDIN'S EGGPLANT NECKLACE

Nasruddin was traveling with a large caravan full of strangers. To make it easy for everyone to recognize him, he wore a string of eggplants around his neck. Everyone started calling him "Mr. Eggplant," but at least they all knew at a glance who he was.

One night the person sleeping on the ground next to Nasruddin decided to play a joke. He took Nasruddin's eggplant necklace and put it around his own neck.

When Nasruddin woke up, he saw the eggplant necklace around the other man's neck.

"If that is me," he thought to himself, "then who am I?"

28. NASRUDDIN VISITS A TOWN FOR THE FIRST TIME

Nasruddin was visiting a new town for the first time. He didn't know anybody in the town, and he wasn't sure what to do or where to go; it made him feel uneasy.

He decided to enter the first door he found open: a carpenter's shop.

"Hello!" said the carpenter.

"Hello!" replied Nasruddin. "Did you see me just now walk into your shop?"

"Yes," replied the carpenter, not sure what Nasruddin was getting at.

"And have you ever seen me before?" asked Nasruddin.

"No, I've never seen you before," admitted the carpenter.

"Then how did you know it was me?"

29. THE SKY IN A DISTANT LAND

Nasruddin went on a long journey to visit a friend who now lived in a distant city.

As they sat up on the roof of his friend's house enjoying the coolness of the night air, Nasruddin stared up at the stars in amazement. "Oooh!" said Nasruddin. "Ahhh!"

Then he looked at his friend and said, "How do you think they did that?"

"How did who do what?" asked Nasruddin's friend, baffled by Nasruddin's reaction.

"The sky painters!" Nasruddin replied. "How were they able to make such a perfect copy here of the sky that I see each night at home?"

30. NASRUDDIN RESCUES THE MOON

Nasruddin was walking home late one night when he stopped at a well to drink some water.

As he stared down into the well, he saw the moon.

"Hang on, Moon!" he shouted. "I'll rescue you!"

He lowered the bucket into the well but, as he tried to maneuver the bucket into just the right spot so the moon could climb in, he stumbled on the hem of his robe and fell over backwards.

He then saw the moon up in the sky.

"I did it!" he exclaimed happily. "You need to be careful you don't fall down again, Moon!"

31. THE SUN OR THE MOON?

There was an argument going on at the coffeehouse, as usual. This time, Nasruddin and his friends were arguing about the sun and the moon.

"Which do you think is more valuable," Nasruddin asked, "the sun, or the moon?"

"What a stupid question, Nasruddin!" they all shouted at him. "The sun is more valuable by far!"

Nasruddin shook his head. "I disagree."

"Are you saying the moon is more valuable than the sun? How can that be?" they asked.

"Isn't it obvious?" Nasruddin replied. "The moon is more valuable because we need the light more at night when it's dark."

32. NASRUDDIN'S HOUSE CATCHES FIRE

Nasruddin's house happened to catch on fire while Nasruddin was in the coffeehouse. One of his neighbors came bursting in to tell him the bad news.

"Nasruddin!" he shouted. "Come quickly! Your house is on fire!"

Nasruddin jumped up and ran to see what had happened. It was true: his house really was on fire. Flames were shooting up into the air and the whole structure was about to collapse.

Nasruddin, however, just stood there smiling.

"What can you be smiling about?" his neighbor asked.

Nasruddin replied, "Don't you see? I've finally gotten rid of those damn bedbugs at last!"

33. THE WISDOM OF CAMELS

Nasruddin was in the coffeehouse with his friends, and the subject of camels came up. Specifically, they started arguing about whether camels were intelligent or not.

"Camels are very intelligent!" exclaimed Nasruddin. "In fact, I would say that camels are more intelligent than people are."

"What makes you say so?" asked one of Nasruddin's friends.

"A camel carries heavy loads, but he never asks for another load in addition to what he carries," replied Nasruddin. "Most people, on the other hand, no matter how heavily burdened they might be already, are always eager to take on new obligations and responsibilities."

34. NASRUDDIN AND THE FISH

Nasruddin and his friends were sitting in the coffeehouse, getting into arguments as usual.

"Fish are truly remarkable animals," Nasruddin opined. "Nobody really respects fish, but they deserve our respect. Talented, intelligent, well-behaved. In fact, there's nothing a person can do that a fish can't do better!"

"That's ridiculous!" protested one of Nasruddin's friends. "Fish can't talk better than people do. Fish can't even talk at all. I've seen hundreds of fish, thousands of fish, but not a single talking fish, and that's because fish can't talk."

"And when you are under the water," Nasruddin replied, "you can't talk either!"

35. HOW OLD IS NASRUDDIN?

Nasruddin was sitting in the coffeehouse drinking coffee with one of his friends. They were talking about this and that, and Nasruddin's friend asked, "Just how old are you, Nasruddin?"

"I'm fifty years old," replied Nasruddin, taking a sip of his coffee.

His friend thought for a moment and then said, "Fifty years old? Really? I'm sure that's what you told me when I asked you your age several years ago."

"That's right. I said I was fifty years old then, and I'm sticking to my story!" said Nasruddin. "I'm a man of my word; you can count on it."

36. NASRUDDIN AND THE STRANGER

A stranger approached Nasruddin as he was standing at the crossroads.

"Which way to town?" the stranger asked.

Nasruddin pointed to the right.

"And how long will it take to get there?"

Nasruddin stared at the stranger intently and shrugged.

"I know you can hear me!" the stranger shouted. "How long will it take me to get to town?"

Nasruddin shrugged again, and the stranger stomped off angrily.

A minute later, Nasruddin shouted, "About half an hour."

The stranger turned and shouted back, "Why didn't you say so?"

"I had to see how quickly you were walking," Nasruddin replied, smiling.

37. NASRUDDIN IN THE ROSE GARDEN

As Nasruddin was walking home one day, he decided to take the long way through a rose garden instead of the usual road. The roses were all in bloom, and the scent was heavenly.

But as Nasruddin strolled through the garden, he slipped in the mud and crashed into some rose bushes. He was badly bruised and bleeding from where the thorns had scratched him, plus he was covered with mud.

Even so, Nasruddin was not distressed. "If misfortune can befall me in this lovely rose garden," he thought, "just imagine the disasters that awaited me on the open road!"

38. NASRUDDIN AND THE EAGLE

Nasruddin was chopping wood one day, working up quite a sweat. Finally he got so hot that he took off his turban and hung it carefully on a tree branch.

Then, without warning, an enormous eagle came swooping down from the sky and snatched Nasruddin's turban.

"Hey, that bird took my turban!" Nasruddin shouted as the eagle soared away up into the sky.

Then he sighed. "Well, I wish he hadn't taken my turban, but I suppose it's all for the best. If I hadn't taken off my turban just in time, the eagle would have carried me away too!"

39. DIFFERENT PEOPLE, DIFFERENT PATHS

Over time, Nasruddin had become famous for his wisdom and learning. As a result people came from near and far to ask him questions.

"I have a question, Nasruddin!" one visitor said. "Why is it that people choose to follow so many different paths in life instead of following the one true path?"

"It's actually for the good of the world that everyone follows their own path," Nasruddin replied. "Just imagine: if everyone followed the same path and ended up at the same destination, the world would lose its balance, tip over, and we would all plunge into the abyss."

40. NASRUDDIN'S BURIED TREASURE

One of Nasruddin's neighbors noticed him in the yard digging a hole. When he went to find out just what Nasruddin was doing, he saw that Nasruddin had dug many holes here and there.

"Why are you digging all these holes?" the neighbor asked.

Nasruddin stared at him wild-eyed. "I'm trying to find the money I buried here last year! Now I really need the money, but I can't find the spot where I buried it."

"Didn't you use something to mark the spot?"

"I did!" said Nasruddin. "I buried it under a cloud that looked just like an elephant."

41. NASRUDDIN IS PERPLEXED

A neighbor saw Nasruddin standing under a tree, scratching his head and looking perplexed.

"Is something wrong?" his neighbor asked.

"I'm puzzled," said Nasruddin. "I've been standing here for hours, and I just can't figure it out."

"Figure what out?" asked his neighbor.

"Don't you see the problem? There's a fish perching up there on that tree branch. Just look!"

Nasruddin pointed, and his neighbor looked up to see.

"I don't understand," said the neighbor. "How can there be a fish perching in a tree that looks just like a parrot?"

"That is exactly what has me puzzled!" replied Nasruddin.

42. NASRUDDIN THE OPTIMIST

Nasruddin's neighbor saw him kneeling by the side of the lake, spooning something into the water. He was used to Nasruddin behaving strangely, but this was unusual even for Nasruddin. He decided to go investigate and see what Nasruddin was doing.

As the neighbor got closer, he saw that Nasruddin was spooning yogurt into the lake.

"Why are you spooning yogurt into the lake?" asked the neighbor.

"It's starter!" Nasruddin explained. "I am hoping to turn the whole lake into yogurt."

"But that's impossible!" said his neighbor.

"Yes, it's impossible," admitted Nasruddin. "But just imagine how wonderful it would be!"

43. NASRUDDIN DIGS A HOLE

Nasruddin's neighbor saw him digging a deep hole in the yard. Nasruddin was barely visible but his neighbor could see shovelfuls of earth flying up out of the hole.

"Nasruddin!" he shouted. "What are you digging that hole for?"

Nasruddin clambered up out of the hole. "I need a place to bury all the rubbish left over from building the new barn."

"And what are you going to do with this heap of earth from the hole you're digging here now?"

Nasruddin paused and scratched his head. "I hadn't thought about that. I suppose I'll have to dig another hole!"

44. NASRUDDIN THE PROUD FATHER

Nasruddin was running through the town square.

A friend noticed him and said, "Nasruddin! Wait a moment and talk! I haven't seen you in such a long time."

"I really don't have time to stop and talk," Nasruddin explained. "I went out to do the shopping, and now I need to hurry home."

"Why the rush?"

"My wife just had a baby!" Nasruddin said proudly.

"What wonderful news!" replied his friend. "I'm very glad for you. And is it a boy or a girl?"

Nasruddin stared at him in amazement. "Yes, it is!" he answered. "But how did you know?"

45. NASRUDDIN IN THE DARK

Night had come on quickly, and Nasruddin and his wife had forgotten to light a candle. Thus, they found themselves sitting in their house in the dark.

“It’s dark, husband,” Nasruddin’s wife said to him. “We need to light a candle.”

“I agree!” said Nasruddin. “It’s completely dark. I can’t see a thing!”

“Well, I’m sure there’s a candle over there on the table to your left. Hand me the candle and I’ll light it.”

“I don’t think that will work,” said Nasruddin. “How do you expect me to tell my left from my right in the dark like this?”

46. NASRUDDIN'S SENSE OF ECONOMY

Nasruddin was acting even more strangely than usual. He had put a patch over one eye and stuffed cotton in one nostril and in one ear. He had also tied one arm behind his back and was hopping on just one leg.

"Nasruddin!" shouted his wife. "Are you alright? What's happened to you?"

"I'm fine!" replied Nasruddin. "I was just thinking that since I have two eyes and two ears and two nostrils, plus two arms and two legs, I should save one of each for future use. That way, I won't use them both up at the same time."

47. WHAT THE QUARREL WAS ABOUT

Nasruddin and his wife awoke to the sound of men quarreling outside. The shouting got louder and louder.

"I'll go see what they are quarreling about," said Nasruddin.

He then lit a lamp and went downstairs.

His wife heard him open the front door. Almost immediately, the shouting stopped. She wondered what Nasruddin had said to stop the quarrel so quickly.

"What happened?" she asked when he came back to bed.

"When I opened the door, one of them grabbed my lamp, and then they both ran off," Nasruddin replied. "I suppose they must have been quarreling about my lamp!"

48. NASRUDDIN'S LOST KEY

Nasruddin was walking around his yard, peering down at the ground and muttering to himself.

Nasruddin's wife came out and asked him, "Did you lose something?"

"I've lost my key," said Nasruddin.

"I'll help you look," said his wife.

Some time passed, and his wife was ready to give up. "Do you have any idea just where exactly you might have dropped it?" she asked.

"I dropped it somewhere in the basement," Nasruddin replied, not looking up.

"Then why are you looking for it out here?" she exclaimed.

"It's dark in the basement," Nasruddin said. "There's more light out here."

49. NASRUDDIN'S TOOTHACHE

Nasruddin had a terrible toothache. It had been hurting for days, getting worse every day. It hurt when he lay down; it hurt when he was standing up. He tried putting warm compresses on it, but that did not help. Warm salt water did not help either.

Nasruddin's wife felt sorry for him at first, but she eventually lost her patience. "If that were my tooth," she finally told him, "I would go have it removed."

"If it were your tooth, I'd have it removed too!" Nasruddin shouted back at her. "The problem is that it's my tooth, not yours."

50. NINE MONTHS FOR A BABY

Nasruddin's wife had given birth to a child barely three months after their wedding.

"Pardon me for asking," said Nasruddin, "but doesn't it usually take nine months for babies to be born?"

"That's right," she replied.

"But then how could you have had this child so soon?" he asked.

"It's simple arithmetic," she answered. "How long have you been married to me?"

"Three months."

"And how long have I been married to you?"

"Three months."

"And how long has the baby been growing inside me?"

"Three months."

"There you go!" she concluded triumphantly. "Nine months, just as it should be."

51. NASRUDDIN'S WIFE AND THE STEW

"Here are four kilos of meat," Nasruddin told his wife. "Please make a nice stew! I'm going out now to invite all my friends."

Nasruddin's wife made the stew but it smelled so good that she invited her friends over, and they ate all the stew.

When Nasruddin got home, his wife shouted, "That cat gobbled the meat before I could cook it!"

Nasruddin looked at her suspiciously. He grabbed the cat and put it on the scales.

"Four kilos!" he said. "So, if this is the cat, where's the meat? And if this is the meat, where's the cat?"

52. HOW OLD IS NASRUDDIN'S WIFE?

One evening Nasruddin turned to his wife and asked, "How old are you?"

"I don't know," she replied.

"What do you mean you don't know? You keep track of everything!" Nasruddin exclaimed. "You know how many knives and forks we have, and how many pots and pans. You could probably tell me how many grains of rice there are in the pantry. How can you not know how old you are?"

"I keep household accounts so that I'll know if someone steals something," she replied. "But nobody is going to steal my age, so what's the point in keeping track?"

53. NO ROOM IN THE BED

Nasruddin and his wife had a very small bed. One night, Nasruddin's wife couldn't take it anymore. "You're not giving me any space at all!" she shouted. "Get up and go! Just go!"

"Go where?" Nasruddin asked, barely awake.

"I don't care! I just need some space in the bed so I can sleep."

Nasruddin started walking.

Eventually, he ran into the nightwatchman who was patrolling the town.

"What are you doing out in the middle of the night?" he asked.

"I'm giving my wife some space," Nasruddin explained. "Could you please go ask her if this is far enough?"

54. ITCHING AND SCRATCHING

Nasruddin and his wife lived in a small house and shared a small bed; they had just a single pillow.

One night Nasruddin's head itched so badly that the itchy feeling woke him up. He scratched and scratched, but it didn't do any good. "What an itch!" he thought to himself.

Then his wife yelled, "Stop scratching my head! I'm trying to sleep."

"My apologies, dearest," said Nasruddin. "Go back to sleep."

Nasruddin then felt around until he found his own head.

"Ah," he said to himself, happily scratching the itch. "That explains it. I was scratching the wrong head."

55. IS SOMEONE SNORING?

Nasruddin's wife complained that she couldn't sleep. "How can anybody sleep with all that loud snoring!" she said.

"I have no idea what you're talking about," Nasruddin replied. "Nothing is disturbing my sleep! But if it will make you feel better, I'll stay awake tonight and investigate."

In the morning he informed his wife of the results. "I didn't hear any snoring," Nasruddin declared. "I stayed awake all night listening, and there wasn't anybody snoring. So, my dear, the only logical conclusion is that you dreamed about someone snoring. To improve your sleep, I'd advise you to dream more softly."

56. SPOUSES, PAST AND PRESENT

Nasruddin's wife died, and eventually he married again. The woman he married was also widowed.

One night as they were lying in bed, Nasruddin's wife began to reminisce about her late husband. "He was so strong, and so handsome!" she said. Then she added, "Unlike some people I know."

"My late wife," said Nasruddin, "was so beautiful, and such a good cook." Then he added, "Unlike some people I know."

As they quarreled, the bed suddenly collapsed underneath them, throwing them both on the floor.

"I didn't think our bed would be strong enough to hold four people," Nasruddin observed.

57. THE SOUND OF A CLOAK

Nasruddin and his wife were arguing loudly, and the neighbors heard everything, as usual.

But then there was a loud bump bump bump and finally a big thump.

The arguing stopped after that, and the neighbors wondered what had happened.

The next day one of the neighbors said to Nasruddin, "What happened last night? Is everything okay at your house?"

"Everything's fine!" Nasruddin replied. "My wife just threw my cloak down the stairs."

"I didn't think a cloak could have made that much noise," said the neighbor.

"Well," Nasruddin admitted, "I happened to be wearing the cloak at the time."

58. NASRUDDIN'S TWO WIVES

Nasruddin had two wives and he loved them both, but they were very jealous of one another, always competing for his affections.

In order to make peace in the house, Nasruddin got two identical green ribbons. He took each wife aside in private and gave her one of the ribbons. "Wear this under your clothes, but secretly; don't show or tell anyone."

The next time the two wives ambushed him, asking which of them he loved more, Nasruddin smiled and said, "All I will say is that the one wearing the green ribbon is the one I love the most."

59. WHO WILL FEED THE DONKEY?

Nasruddin and his wife were arguing about whose turn it was to feed the donkey. Finally they agreed: whoever spoke the next word would have to go feed the donkey.

So, neither one spoke a word all day.

And neither one spoke a word all evening.

In the night, a thief came and broke into their house.

Nasruddin saw him carrying away their clothes, their furniture, everything, but he said nothing at all.

In the morning, his wife saw what had happened and yelled, "We've been robbed!"

Nasruddin laughed in triumph. "And now you have to go feed the donkey!"

60. THE BURGLAR IN THE WELL

Nasruddin awoke to the sound of a burglar outside. He crept into the yard but saw nobody, and then he looked in the well. Sure enough, he saw a man's face in the water.

"Don't you even think about trying to escape!" he shouted down at the burglar.

He then rushed inside to get dressed. "I'll fetch the police!" he said. "You go keep an eye on the burglar in the well!"

His wife hurried outside and peered down into the well.

"Oh, I see another one!" she shouted. "He must have brought his wife with him as an accomplice."

61. THE BREAD IN THE POND

Nasruddin's son was walking by the pond eating some bread. When he leaned over to look in the water, the bread fell out of his hand.

Then he saw that another boy in the pond had taken his bread, so he ran home crying and told his father what had happened. "Someone in the pond stole my bread!" he sobbed.

Nasruddin went to the pond and looked in the water. He saw a bearded man, about his own age.

"Hey there, old man!" he shouted. "You ought to be ashamed of yourself, stealing bread from a little boy like that."

62. NASRUDDIN WAS ROBBED

Nasruddin and his wife returned home after a long journey to find that robbers had broken into their home and stolen everything.

Of course, everyone had their own opinion about what had happened.

"You probably forgot to lock the door!" Nasruddin's wife exclaimed.

"I told you to put bars on the windows!" said a friend.

"Leaving the house unattended for such a long time is very risky!" observed a neighbor.

Everyone chimed in, and they all blamed Nasruddin.

Finally, Nasruddin couldn't take it anymore and shouted, "Is there no one here who will put the blame on the actual robbers?"

63. NASRUDDIN IN THE CUPBOARD

During the night, Nasruddin heard robbers ransacking his house, so he quietly crept downstairs and hid in the cupboard. He then listened as the robbers worked their way through the house, cursing and swearing. They were not able to find anything worth stealing, and Nasruddin could tell they were getting more and more angry.

Finally, one of the robbers opened the cupboard door and discovered Nasruddin there, cowering in his nightshirt.

"What are you doing in this cupboard?" the robber yelled at him.

"I'm hiding here in shame," said Nasruddin apologetically, "because there is nothing worth stealing in my house."

64. THE BURGLAR IN THE DARK

Nasruddin awoke to the sound of a burglar in his house. He got up, crept downstairs, and found the burglar stuffing all kinds of household objects into his sack.

"Excuse me," said Nasruddin, startling the burglar, who stared at Nasruddin in surprise.

"It's dark now, of course," continued Nasruddin, "so it's entirely possible you don't realize what you're doing. You seem to think these objects have some kind of value. But the fact is that they don't have any value at all. I've seen these objects in broad daylight, and I can assure you that everything here is completely worthless."

65. BAGS OF LOOT

Nasruddin's wife woke him in the middle of the night. "I heard burglars!" she whispered. "I saw them leaving their bags of loot in the garden, and then I heard them come into our house. It sounds like they're in the kitchen."

Nasruddin leaped out of bed, pulled on his clothes, and began to climb out of the bedroom window into the garden.

"What are you doing?" his wife asked.

"I'm going to sneak outside," Nasruddin whispered, "and steal the loot from other people's houses while the thieves waste their time looking for something worth stealing here inside our house."

66. THE THIEF WITH A WAGON

Nasruddin and his wife had been visiting relatives and arrived back home just as a thief was loading the last of their furniture into a wagon.

“Let’s follow him!” Nasruddin whispered to his wife.

When the thief arrived at his own house, he began unloading Nasruddin’s furniture.

“I’ll give you a hand!” Nasruddin said. “Wife, go see if there’s something to eat in the kitchen.”

“Hey!” said the thief. “What do you think you’re doing?”

“Isn’t this our new house?” asked Nasruddin. “I saw all our furniture on your wagon and thought you were moving us to a new house.”

67. THE THIEF AND NASRUDDIN'S ROOSTER

Nasruddin heard squawking from the henhouse during the night. "It must be a thief," he thought, and he ran outside, where he found a man creeping away from the henhouse.

By the light of the moon, Nasruddin could clearly see a rooster's tail-feathers sticking out from under the man's cloak.

"Give me back my rooster, you thief!" shouted Nasruddin.

The man stood up straight and answered back, "Sir, please believe me! I have absolutely no idea what you're talking about."

"And do you think I'm going to believe you," Nasruddin replied, "or am I going to believe the rooster's tail-feathers?"

68. NASRUDDIN AND THE THIEF'S SHOES

Nasruddin awoke when he heard a thief in his house. He crept downstairs and saw the thief had politely left his shoes by the door. Nasruddin grabbed the shoes, and then shouted, "Thief! Thief!"

The thief ran to the door and, when he saw his shoes were gone, he dashed barefoot into the street.

Nasruddin chased him, shouting, "Thief! Thief!"

People rushed out of their houses and easily caught the criminal.

"This is not fair!" the thief protested. "This is not right!"

Then he pointed at Nasruddin accusingly. "I took nothing from that man's house, but he stole my shoes!"

69. NASRUDDIN AND THE APPLE TREE

As he was riding past an apple orchard, Nasruddin was seized by a desire for apples, so he led his donkey up to one of the trees.

Then, standing on the donkey's back, he reached up and grabbed hold of a branch.

Just as he was about to pick an apple, though, the orchard's owner came running up. This startled the donkey, who bolted and left Nasruddin dangling from the branch.

"Get down from there!" the man shouted. "I'm going to have you arrested for stealing my apples!"

"I'm no thief," Nasruddin shouted back. "I just fell off my donkey."

70. NASRUDDIN AND THE WIND

Nasruddin was raiding a garden when the garden's owner caught him in the act.

"What are you doing?" shouted the owner.

"Well, you see," said Nasruddin, trying to think of an explanation, "I was blown here by the wind."

"What about all those vegetables lying here that someone has pulled up out of the ground?"

"I grabbed hold of those vegetables to stop my flight," Nasruddin replied.

"And what about that big bag full of vegetables you are holding in your hand?"

"This is ballast," said Nasruddin, "in case the wind starts blowing and tries to carry me off again!"

71. NASRUDDIN THE NIGHTINGALE

Nasruddin had broken into an apricot orchard and climbed a tree.

As he was stuffing his pockets with apricots, the owner of the orchard discovered him.

"What are you doing up in that tree?" the man shouted.

Nasruddin said nothing.

"I repeat: what are you doing up there?"

"Are you talking to me?" asked Nasruddin.

"Yes, you!"

"I'm just a nightingale," said Nasruddin. "This tree is my home."

"If you're a nightingale, sing!" said the man.

Nasruddin sang. He sang very badly.

"You don't sound like a nightingale!"

"I'm a young nightingale," said Nasruddin. "I'm still just learning to sing."

72. NASRUDDIN'S LADDER

Nasruddin was fond of fruit, and he was also fond of raiding his neighbor's orchards.

One night he had just lowered a ladder into someone's orchard in order to raid it, but the orchard's owner caught him in the act.

"What are you doing with that ladder?" the man shouted at him.

"Are you talking about this ladder?" asked Nasruddin. "Well, to tell the truth, I'm just trying to sell this ladder."

"You can't sell a ladder here!" the man replied.

"I beg to differ," said Nasruddin indignantly. "A ladder can be sold anywhere! Do you want to buy it?"

73. NASRUDDIN AND THE TAILOR

Nasruddin went into a tailor's shop. "I'd like to try on a pair of trousers."

The tailor gave him the trousers, and Nasruddin tried them on.

"They're not quite right," he said, giving them back to the tailor. "I'd like to try a jacket now, please."

Nasruddin liked the jacket very much. "I'll take it!" he said, and then he began to walk out the door.

"But wait!" shouted the tailor. "You haven't paid!"

"I exchanged the trousers for the jacket," Nasruddin explained.

"But you didn't pay for the trousers!"

"Of course not!" said Nasruddin. "I didn't want the trousers!"

74. NASRUDDIN AND THE PORTER

Nasruddin needed to hire a porter to take home four large sacks of grain he had bought at the market.

Just outside the market, he found a porter with a wagon.

"Good day, sir!" said Nasruddin.

"Good day to you!" replied the porter.

"How much will you charge to take me and my purchases to my house?" Nasruddin asked.

"That will be four copper coins for you," said the porter. "No charge for the purchases."

"Excellent!" said Nasruddin as he started heaving the sacks of grain onto the wagon. "You just take my purchases home, and I'll follow on foot."

75. NASRUDDIN AND THE WEALTHY MERCHANT

Nasruddin once found himself traveling in the company of a wealthy merchant.

"The more wealthy I am, the more wealthy I become," said the merchant proudly. "Look at my fine boots and your shabby sandals, my thoroughbred horse and your broken-down donkey, my elegant garments and your threadbare cloak..."

As the merchant was speaking, robbers suddenly rode up and attacked them, stripping the merchant of his clothes and stealing his horse. Meanwhile, they ignored Nasruddin and his donkey.

"Remarkable!" said Nasruddin, "The more wealthy you were, the more you had to lose, while my circumstances remain the same as before."

76. DONKEYS AND HORSES

Nasruddin was riding his donkey along the road when a rich man on a fine horse rode up alongside him.

"I've been watching you and your donkey," he said, "and you are a sorry-looking sight. I don't know who looks more pathetic: you or your donkey!"

Nasruddin did not reply.

"I'm talking to you!" shouted the rich man. "Don't you have anything to say?"

"Excuse me," said Nasruddin apologetically. "I was just so surprised that I didn't know what to say."

"What do you mean you were surprised?"

Nasruddin smiled. "I've never actually seen a donkey riding a horse before!"

77. THE CABBAGE AND THE COOKING-POT

Nasruddin and his friends were sitting in the coffeehouse, boasting.

"I once grew a cucumber as long as my arm," one man said.

"That's nothing!" said another. "I once grew a watermelon as big as a sheep."

"Ha!" said another. "I've got you both beat: I once grew a head of cabbage that was as large as an elephant."

Then Nasruddin said, "Just yesterday I bought a cooking-pot as big as a polo field."

"That's ridiculous!" the men shouted at Nasruddin. "Why would anyone want a pot that big?"

"In order to cook that head of cabbage!" replied Nasruddin, smiling.

78. JOKES IN THE COFFEEHOUSE

Nasruddin and his friends were sitting in the coffeehouse, and one of them decided to tell a joke. It was a very long joke, and the man told the joke very badly.

Everyone squirmed in their seats as they listened to his performance.

Finally, the joker reached the punchline, which he bungled.

No one laughed… except Nasruddin.

Later, one of Nasruddin's friends asked him, "Why did you laugh at that joke? It wasn't funny at all."

"You should always laugh at the joke," Nasruddin told him. "If you don't, there's a possibility that they might try to tell it again."

79. A TOKEN OF FRIENDSHIP

One of Nasruddin's dearest friends was moving away to a distant city.

"I'll miss you," said Nasruddin's friend.

"I'll miss you too," Nasruddin replied.

"Hey, I've got an idea!" said his friend. "Why don't you give me that gold ring of yours as a memento? Then, whenever I look at that ring on my finger, I'll remember that you gave it to me."

Nasruddin thought for a moment.

"I've got a better idea," he said. "I won't give you my gold ring, and that way whenever you look at your finger, you'll remember that I didn't give it to you."

80. GETTING FOOLED BY NASRUDDIN

Nasruddin had a friend he'd known for a long time.

"You're quite the trickster," Nasruddin's friend said, "but I've seen all your tricks. You can fool everybody else, but you can't fool me."

Nasruddin scratched his head thoughtfully and then he said, "Wait here! I think I know a way to fool you. I'll be right back!"

"Okay," the man agreed. "You can try if you want, but I'm going to be on my guard!"

The man stood there and waited.

And waited.

And as he was waiting, he realized ... Nasruddin wasn't coming back.

Nasruddin had fooled him after all.

81. NASRUDDIN ON THE ROOF

A man down on the ground was shouting to Nasruddin up on the roof. "Please, sir, come here!"

Nasruddin climbed down and asked the man what he wanted.

"I need money," the man explained.

"Why didn't you just say so?" said Nasruddin. "Instead, you made me climb down."

"I was embarrassed to shout it out loud," the man explained.

Nasruddin told the man to come up on the roof. Then, once they were both up on the roof, Nasruddin told the man he had nothing to give him.

"Why didn't you just say so?" the man asked.

Nasruddin just smiled.

82. AN UNEXPECTED VISIT FROM NASRUDDIN

Nasruddin decided to pay his friend an unexpected visit.

From the upstairs window, the man could see Nasruddin coming. "It's Nasruddin!" he shouted to his wife. "Tell him I'm not home."

When Nasruddin knocked at the door, the man's wife answered. "My husband has gone out," she said apologetically. "He's not here right now."

Nasruddin looked up and saw the man in the upstairs window.

"Please tell him that I called," Nasruddin said. "And you might also let him know that when he goes out, he should take his head with him instead of hanging it there in the window."

83. NASRUDDIN EATING EGGS

Nasruddin was sitting in a chair outside, eating eggs for dinner. He didn't usually eat dinner outside, and eggs were not his usual dinner, but so it was: Nasruddin was sitting in a chair outside, eating eggs for dinner.

One of Nasruddin's neighbors happened to walk by, and he just couldn't keep quiet. "Hey there, Nasruddin," he said, "why are you sitting in your chair eating eggs like that?"

Nasruddin looked up and replied, "Would it be better if I sat in the eggs and ate the chair?"

The best way to answer a foolish question is with another question.

84. NASRUDDIN AND THE PHILOSOPHER'S QUESTIONS

A renowned philosopher traveled to Nasruddin's town to challenge him in a contest of wisdom. Everyone gathered to see the show, hoping that Nasruddin would uphold the honor of their town.

To begin the contest, the challenger asked if Nasruddin wanted to answer one hundred easy questions or just one hard question.

"I'll take the one hard question," Nasruddin said.

"Which came first: the chicken or the egg?"

"The chicken," replied Nasruddin confidently.

The philosopher was surprised by Nasruddin's answer. "How can you be so sure?"

"Ah," said Nasruddin, "that is your second question. I agreed to answer only one."

85. NASRUDDIN REWARDS HIS SON

Nasruddin's son received a good report from his teacher at school.

"Son, I'm proud of you," said Nasruddin. "You may make a request of me, and I will grant it."

The son was taken aback by this generous offer. "May I have a day to think about it?" he asked.

"Yes," said Nasruddin.

The boy came back the next day and said, "Father, I want a donkey."

"Well, that would be two requests now, wouldn't it? I already granted your request for a day to think things over."

Nasruddin's son was disappointed, but not surprised: he should have known better!

86. NASRUDDIN GETS A HAIRCUT

Nasruddin and a little boy walked into a barbershop together. "Do me first, and then the boy here," Nasruddin said.

The barber gave Nasruddin a haircut and as he was giving the boy a haircut, Nasruddin strolled out of the shop.

When he had finished, the barber waited for Nasruddin to come back and pay.

Finally he asked the boy, "When do you think your father will be back?"

"Oh, that's not my father," said the boy. "He just picked me up off the street out there and said, 'Let's go get us some free haircuts' … and so we did!"

87. NASRUDDIN AND THE TALL TREE

The village boys wanted to trick Nasruddin and steal his new shoes.

"Look at this tall tree!" they shouted. "We're too small to climb it, but maybe you can."

Nasruddin looked at the tree, smiled and said, "That would be fun. I'll try!"

So, Nasruddin took off his new shoes. Next, he tucked the shoes inside his belt. Then he began climbing.

"Wait!" shouted the boys. "Why are you taking your shoes with you?"

"This tree is so tall that it might lead all the way to heaven," Nasruddin replied, "and I'll need my shoes to walk around up there."

88. NASRUDDIN'S PLAYFUL TURBAN

It was a windy day and as Nasruddin was walking home, a big gust of wind blew the turban right off his head. Some children who were playing nearby grabbed the turban and began tossing it back and forth.

Nasruddin chased the children, hoping to get his turban back. "Hey there, children!" he said. "Give me back my turban!"

Then, when he saw how much fun the children were having, he gave up and went home.

"Where's your turban?" Nasruddin's wife asked. "Did you leave it somewhere?"

"It suddenly remembered its childhood," replied Nasruddin, "and it decided to go play."

89. YOUNG NASRUDDIN AND THE TALL TALES

When he was a young boy, Nasruddin liked to sit around the fires of the passing caravans and listen to travelers' tales about faraway places. He enjoyed the stories of valiant warriors in battle, tales of genies and magic, and most of all he enjoyed the anecdotes about the very strange habits of people who lived in distant lands.

"I once visited a land that was so hot all year long," one traveler claimed, "that no one in their country wore any clothes."

"Impossible!" protested Nasruddin. "Without clothes, how would you be able to tell the men from the women?"

90. NAKED NASRUDDIN

One morning Nasruddin arrived at school not wearing any clothes. He was completely naked! All the other schoolboys laughed at him, but the teacher was not amused. In fact, he was very angry.

"Nasruddin, explain yourself!" said the teacher sternly. "What on earth are you doing here without any clothes on?"

"Just let me explain," Nasruddin replied, smiling brightly at the teacher. "I woke up late, so I was in a big hurry and I ran just as fast as I could. I simply didn't have time to get dressed if I wanted to get here to school on time."

91. NASRUDDIN AND THE VILLAGE BOYS

Nasruddin met some boys from the village and decided to play a trick on them.

"Hey!" he shouted. "Did you know it's the mayor's birthday? There's a party with music and dancing and all the food you can eat. You better hurry and run to the mayor's house as fast as you can!"

"Thank you, Nasruddin!" shouted the boys, and they immediately dashed off towards the mayor's house.

Then Nasruddin thought to himself, "You know, it really might be the mayor's birthday after all…" and he began to run after the boys.

"Wait for me!" he shouted. "I'm coming too!"

92. NASRUDDIN AND THE GRAPES

Nasruddin was on his way home carrying a basket full of bunches of grapes when he ran into some children along the way.

"Give us some grapes, Nasruddin!" shouted the children. "Please, Nasruddin, share your grapes with us!"

Nasruddin really didn't want to share his grapes with the children, but the children insisted.

Reluctantly, he took some grapes from the basket and cut each grape in half. He then gave each child half a grape.

"Give us more!" the children complained.

"All the grapes in this basket taste the same," Nasruddin explained. "Half of a grape is all you need."

93. NASRUDDIN AND THE SUGAR

A mother brought her son to see Nasruddin. “My son eats too much sugar,” she said. “Please make him stop!”

Nasruddin patted the boy on the head and said, “Come back in two weeks and we’ll see what we can do.”

The mother promised to return in two weeks.

At their next meeting, Nasruddin looked at the boy and said sternly, “You must stop eating sugar!”

“Why did we have to wait two weeks for you to say that?” asked the mother.

“I had to make myself stop eating sugar,” replied Nasruddin, “before telling someone else to do the same.”

94. NASRUDDIN AND THE HOOLIGAN

One of the local hooligans threw a rock at Nasruddin's donkey. Nasruddin saw what the boy had done but, instead of yelling at him, he laughed.

"You're a very good shot!" Nasruddin exclaimed. "I'm impressed. But my donkey is not a worthy target for someone of your talent. You deserve a better target!"

Nasruddin then noticed the mayor riding by on his horse.

"Like the mayor, for example," Nasruddin said, pointing.

The boy threw a rock at the horse's rump, and when the horse reared, the mayor tumbled to the ground.

"Arrest that boy!" the mayor shouted.

Nasruddin just smiled.

95. NASRUDDIN AND THE DONKEY-BOY

Nasruddin bought a donkey and was leading it home. On the way, a thief stole the donkey and left his young son in the harness.

When he got home, Nasruddin was surprised to see his donkey had turned into a boy.

"For my bad behavior, my mother cursed me to become a donkey," the boy said. "But I repented, and now I'm human again."

"Make sure you don't misbehave in future!" Nasruddin said, sending the boy home.

The next day Nasruddin saw the same donkey at the market. "You bad boy!" said Nasruddin. "Didn't I tell you to behave yourself?"

96. FRIGHTENING NASRUDDIN

"Our son won't do his chores," said Nasruddin's wife. "You must frighten him to make him behave!"

Nasruddin jumped up and began to scream. He stuck out his tongue and shook his fists wildly. He then grabbed a knife.

At this, Nasruddin's wife started sobbing, and Nasruddin himself ran out of the room.

When he returned, his wife was still crying, and his son was hiding under a chair.

"Why did you run away?" she asked.

"I scared even myself," Nasruddin admitted. "Terror easily gets out of control. I meant to frighten our son, and instead I frightened us all."

97. BIG POT, LITTLE POT

Nasruddin borrowed a big cooking pot from his neighbor. When he returned it, he placed a little pot inside the big pot.

"What's this?" asked his neighbor.

"Your big pot gave birth to a little baby pot," Nasruddin explained.

The neighbor laughed, and he kept the little pot.

Nasruddin borrowed the big pot again later, but he didn't return it.

When his neighbor asked for it back, Nasruddin said, "I'm sorry, but your pot died."

"What do you mean it died?" exclaimed the neighbor. "Pots can't die!"

"If pots can give birth, of course they can die," replied Nasruddin, smiling.

98. NASRUDDIN GOES UPSTAIRS

Nasruddin had invited his friends to dinner. "They're coming right behind me," he said to his wife when he got home.

"But there's no food in the house!" she exclaimed.

"What will we do?" groaned Nasruddin.

"Go upstairs! I'll do the rest."

A moment later, Nasruddin's friends knocked at the door. "Your husband invited us for dinner!" they said.

"Alas, my husband has gone out," his wife told them. "I don't know when he'll be back."

"But we saw him come in!"

"I could have gone out the back!" Nasruddin shouted from upstairs. "You didn't think of that, did you?"

99. NASRUDDIN THINKS OF SOUP

Nasruddin was hungry, but he had nothing to eat in the house. He sat in the kitchen, dreaming of soup. A nice noodle soup with beans and lentils, some onion and spinach, seasoned with some turmeric, yogurt on the side…

Then, as Nasruddin was thinking about that soup, he heard a knock at the door. It was his neighbor's young son.

"Please, Nasruddin," said the boy, "if you have cooked a pot of soup here, may we please have some?"

The boy then held out an empty bowl.

"Incredible!" Nasruddin exclaimed. "The neighbors can smell even the thought of soup."

100. NASRUDDIN'S CLOTHESLINE

A neighbor asked to borrow Nasruddin's clothesline.

"I'm afraid that's not possible," said Nasruddin. He tried to sound apologetic, but he really didn't want to loan anything to anyone. "I'm using the clothesline right now."

"But I didn't see any clothes drying outside. What are you using it for?"

"I'm using it to dry flour," Nasruddin explained. "I spilled some water and the flour got wet. The flour is still drying."

"You can't use a clothesline for drying flour!" exclaimed the neighbor. "That's impossible!"

"It's completely possible," Nasruddin replied calmly, "when your purpose is to avoid loaning out your clothesline."

101. NASRUDDIN ASKS THE DONKEY

Nasruddin's neighbor asked to borrow his donkey.

This particular neighbor had a bad temper, and Nasruddin was reluctant to refuse him.

"Let me go ask the donkey," he said.

A few moments later, Nasruddin returned.

"My deepest apologies," he said to his neighbor, "but the donkey refuses. He explained his reasoning like this: if I make him work for you, you are likely to beat him, and if you beat him, he will bite you, and after he bites you, you will curse me. So really, it's better for all of us if I do not loan you the donkey."

102. NASRUDDIN AND THE NEIGHBOR'S DOG

The neighbor's dog bit Nasruddin. After bandaging the wound, Nasruddin went next door to the neighbor to complain.

"That vicious dog of yours just bit me!" Nasruddin shouted.

"I'm very sorry to hear that," said the neighbor. "He's really a very nice dog. Let me go in the kitchen and get some bread. Then you can feed him the bread yourself, and he'll be your friend forever."

"That's a terrible idea!" said Nasruddin. "If I do that, your dog will tell all the other dogs in town, and then all those dogs will come here trying to bite me too."

103. NASRUDDIN AND THE NEIGHBOR'S BULL

Nasruddin's neighbor had a bull, and one day that bull blundered into Nasruddin's garden, trampling all of Nasruddin's vegetables.

When Nasruddin saw what his neighbor's bull had done, he grabbed a whip and chased the bull out of the garden, whipping the bull as he did so.

"You accursed creature!" he shouted. "I'll show you who's the boss here! Take that! And take that!"

The bull bellowed loudly every time he felt the sting of Nasruddin's whip.

"Hey there!" shouted Nasruddin's neighbor. "What are you doing?"

"You stay out of this," replied Nasruddin. "This is between me and the bull!"

104. NASRUDDIN AND THE SESAME SEEDS

As one of Nasruddin's neighbors walked by, he noticed that Nasruddin was throwing sesame seeds onto the ground. There were sesame seeds everywhere!

"What on earth are you doing?" the neighbor asked.

"I'm scattering sesame seeds," Nasruddin replied calmly.

"I can see that!" said his neighbor. "But I don't understand why you're scattering sesame seeds."

"To keep the tigers away," said Nasruddin. "I highly recommend you give it a try too!"

"I still don't understand," his neighbor replied. "There aren't any tigers anywhere near here."

"I know!" Nasruddin exclaimed. "Isn't it wonderful? The sesame seeds are working just as expected."

105. NASRUDDIN AND THE BEARS

A rich man had invited Nasruddin to go with him on a bear hunt. Reluctantly, Nasruddin accepted the invitation.

A few days later, he returned from the hunt beaming with happiness.

"How did it go?" his neighbor asked him.

"It was wonderful!" Nasruddin replied with a smile.

"How many bears did you kill?"

"None!"

"How many bears did you chase?"

"None!"

"How many bears did you see?"

"None!" said Nasruddin happily.

His neighbor stared at him in confusion.

"That is why it was wonderful!" Nasruddin explained. "I don't mind hunting bears if there are not any bears to be found."

106. NASRUDDIN THE ARCHITECT

"Our house is so crowded," Nasruddin's neighbor complained. "We can't stand it anymore."

"I can help," Nasruddin said. "Will you obey my advice exactly?"

His neighbor nodded.

"Bring your goats, chickens, and donkey into the house."

A week later, the neighbor told Nasruddin, "That just made things worse!"

"I know," said Nasruddin. "But now, send the donkey outside."

"That's better," said the neighbor a week later.

"Now send the chickens back out."

"That's much better," the neighbor said next time.

"Now the goats."

Nasruddin's neighbor came back smiling. "Thank you, Nasruddin!" he said. "Our house is so much bigger now!"

107. THE LIGHT IN THE GARDEN

Nasruddin's neighbor was complaining about how dark it was inside his house.

"It's not at all like your nice house here," the neighbor said. "Your house is full of light, but my house is so dark. I don't know what to do."

"I sympathize," Nasruddin replied. "Light is very important." He then thought for a few moments. "How about in your garden?" Nasruddin asked. "Is there light in your garden?"

"Well, of course there's light in the garden. The garden is full of light!"

"Then that's the solution!" exclaimed Nasruddin. "Just move your house into the garden where it's light."

108. THE WARMTH OF A CANDLE

Nasruddin made a bet with his neighbor. “I’ll stand in the snow with only a blanket for warmth. If I last all night, you feed me; otherwise, I feed you.”

Nasruddin stood all night in the snow. “I won!” he shouted.

“No!” his neighbor protested. “You used the candle burning in my window for warmth. I’ll come over tonight to eat that dinner.”

When the neighbor arrived, Nasruddin explained the soup wasn’t ready.

The neighbor waited.

And waited.

Finally, he went into the kitchen and saw a pot suspended over a candle.

“Imagine that!” said Nasruddin. “The soup’s still cold.”

109. NASRUDDIN'S HOUSE WITH MANY WINDOWS

Nasruddin had built a new house, and there were many windows, big and small, in every wall.

"I've never seen a house with so many windows!" said Nasruddin's neighbor.

"That's my own design," Nasruddin explained. "This new house has twenty windows! My old house had just one."

"Why so many?" asked the neighbor.

"To stay warm in winter!" replied Nasruddin. "My old house became much warmer when I closed my window in the winter. Now when winter comes, I have twenty windows to close, so the house will be twenty times warmer. I won't even need to light a fire!"

110. NASRUDDIN AND THE WOOL

Nasruddin owed his neighbor money. "But don't worry," Nasruddin said. "I've got a plan!"

His neighbor looked doubtful. "Do tell!" he said.

"I planted some bramble bushes outside; you probably saw them. And you know how the shepherds drive their flocks down the road on their way to the pasture…? The wool from those passing sheep will get caught on the brambles. I'm going to harvest that wool, sell it, and that's how I will pay you back."

Nasruddin's neighbor burst out laughing. "I don't think you'll ever pay me back," he said, "but at least you keep me entertained!"

111. NASRUDDIN AND THE DENTIST

Nasruddin had been at the dentist all morning, and his wife wondered what was taking so long.

Finally, Nasruddin walked through the door, grinning happily, his mouth wide open.

His wife gasped in shock. "Nasruddin!" she exclaimed. "What has happened to your teeth?"

"Well, you know how much that dentist charges," Nasruddin replied. "He wanted a gold coin to remove my bad tooth. A gold coin! It's outrageous. So we haggled and haggled, back and forth, back and forth, and I finally persuaded him to take out four more teeth. So I got five removed for the price of one!"

112. NASRUDDIN AND THE BAKER

Nasruddin owed the baker money, so when the baker saw Nasruddin on the street, he said, "Come with me!" and he led Nasruddin into the bakery.

"Look!" the baker said, pointing at the account book. "You owe me three silver coins."

Nasruddin nodded, looking at the account book. "I see my brother-in-law owes you five," he remarked. "I was on my way to see him just now; I'll get him to pay also!"

"Excellent!" replied the baker.

"He owes you five, and I owe three," Nasruddin said. "So you can give me two coins now, and that will square things."

113. THE ANGEL WITH THE GOLDEN COINS

Nasruddin had a dream. In his dream, an angel was counting golden coins into Nasruddin's hand, one at a time. One, two, three, four, five, six, seven, eight... finally the angel had counted out nine coins.

"If you could give me ten coins," Nasruddin said to the angel, "I would be able to pay all my debts."

The angel then looked at him angrily and disappeared.

Nasruddin awoke from his dream. He looked, and saw there were no golden coins in his hand.

"Come back, angel!" shouted Nasruddin. "Please come back! I've thought it over, and I'll take the nine!"

114. BUYING AN ELEPHANT

Nasruddin decided he was going to buy an elephant, and he knew it would be an expensive purchase. Since he didn't have enough money, he went to his richest friend to borrow the money.

His friend, however, refused to give him the loan. "You're not thinking clearly, Nasruddin," he said. "Elephants are expensive to buy, and they are also expensive to keep. If you don't have the money to buy an elephant, how will you be able to afford to house the elephant and feed it?"

"You don't understand," said Nasruddin angrily. "I came here for a loan, not advice."

115. WHO WANTS TO GET RICH?

Nasruddin stood in the village square and shouted loudly for all to hear, "Who wants to get rich?"

A few people gathered around. "We do!" they yelled.

"And who wants to get rich without doing any work?"

More people began to gather around. "We do!" they yelled.

"Tell me, people," Nasruddin shouted even more loudly, "who wants the secret to getting rich without having to do any work at all?"

A crowd of people now filled the square. "We do! We all do!" they yelled.

"I do too!" shouted Nasruddin.

Then he added, "Does anybody here actually know the secret?"

116. A LOAN FROM NASRUDDIN

Nasruddin's neighbor needed a loan.

"I'm desperate!" he said. "Can you possibly loan me six hundred silver coins? Then just let me have one month to pay the loan back. One month is all I need, I swear!"

"You want me to give you six hundred silver coins, then a month to pay me back," Nasruddin repeated. "Well, I can do half."

"Bless you! Three hundred will be a big help."

"That's not what I meant," said Nasruddin. "I don't have any money at all to loan you, but you can have a month in which to pay me back."

117. THE PROPER WAY TO BEG

A beggar approached Nasruddin on the street.

"Please, kind sir," he said, "could you possibly give me a coin or two?"

Nasruddin was indignant. "It's not at all proper for a rich man such as myself to give a beggar such a paltry sum."

The beggar bowed apologetically. "Please, kind sir, forgive my mistake," he said. "Could you possibly give me a hundred coins?"

Nasruddin became even more indignant. "It's not at all proper for a beggar like yourself to ask a complete stranger to give him a hundred coins!" he exclaimed.

And with that, Nasruddin continued on his way.

118. THE POOR MAN IN THE COFFEEHOUSE

Nasruddin saw a stranger in the coffeehouse who looked very sad.

"Is something the matter?" Nasruddin asked him.

"I used to be rich!" said the man. "I lived in a mansion, and I had many servants. But I've lost it all: money, mansion, servants, everything. I can barely pay for this coffee. Soon I'll be begging on the streets. I'm sick with worry."

"Oh, you won't have to feel like this for long," Nasruddin assured him.

The man looked at Nasruddin eagerly. "Do you mean I'll get rich again?"

"No," said Nasruddin. "I mean you'll get used to being poor."

119. NASRUDDIN LOOKS FOR WORK

Nasruddin desperately needed a job. He visited every shop, every workshop, every warehouse seeking employment.

Finally, he came to the warehouse of a merchant with a shady reputation.

"Do you have any job openings?" Nasruddin asked.

"Well," said the merchant, "I am looking for a bookkeeper. How's your arithmetic?"

"My arithmetic is excellent!" said Nasruddin enthusiastically.

"I'll have to give you a test first. Are you ready?"

Nasruddin nodded.

"How much is two plus two?"

Nasruddin thought for a moment and then said in a low voice, "How much do you want it to be?"

"You're hired!" said the merchant.

120. NASRUDDIN'S DONKEY FOR SALE

"That wretched donkey of mine ran away again," said Nasruddin. "If he ever comes back, I'll sell him for a single copper coin!"

The donkey came back, and Nasruddin regretted his reckless oath.

So, he took the cat, who was the donkey's playmate, and put the cat in the donkey's saddlebag. Then he went to the market.

"Buy this fine donkey for just one copper coin!" Nasruddin shouted. "But you must buy the cat too; the donkey would be heartbroken without him."

"How much for the cat?" someone asked.

"The cat will cost you one hundred silver coins," Nasruddin replied.

121. NASRUDDIN AT THE BATHHOUSE

Nasruddin went to the bathhouse.

When the attendant saw Nasruddin's shabby clothes, he treated him poorly, giving him a threadbare towel and only a tiny piece of soap. Nevertheless, after Nasruddin finished his bath, he tipped the attendant very generously.

On his next visit, the attendant greeted Nasruddin with great respect, remembering the generous tip. He gave Nasruddin several luxurious towels and a new bar of soap. But when he left, Nasruddin gave the attendant no tip at all.

"That's for last time," Nasruddin explained, "and the tip I gave you last time was for this time. Now we're even!"

122. WHAT A BEGGAR NEEDS

Nasruddin was walking down the street when a beggar accosted him.

"I know you," said Nasruddin. "You like drinking coffee in the coffeehouse, don't you?

The beggar nodded. "Yes, I do."

"And the bathhouse? And drinking with your friends?"

The beggar kept nodding, and Nasruddin gave him a gold coin.

Nasruddin met a second beggar; he had overheard the first conversation.

"What about you?" asked Nasruddin. "The coffeehouse?"

"Never!" said the beggar.

"Bathhouse? Drinking?"

The beggar shook his head emphatically, and Nasruddin gave him a copper coin.

"I don't understand!" complained the beggar.

"Your needs are fewer," replied Nasruddin, smiling.

123. HONORED GUESTS AT THE BANQUET

Nasruddin was invited to a banquet. He rushed off immediately, imagining the fine food he would eat there.

But when he arrived in his shabby clothes, they seated him far from the main table, with nothing but bread to eat.

So Nasruddin ran home, put on his best clothes, and returned to the banquet. This time they seated him at the main table which was loaded with delicious food.

Nasruddin then began rubbing the food all over his clothes.

"What are you doing?" shouted the host.

"I'm feeding my clothes," Nasruddin replied, "as they are the honored guests, not me."

124. NASRUDDIN'S TWO HANDS

Nasruddin was delighted to receive a dinner invitation from his friend.

He arrived early, and hungry, eager to try every single dish.

As the food was served, Nasruddin reached with both hands, grabbing for the meat and the bread, anything and everything he could reach, hurriedly stuffing the food into his mouth.

Finally one of the other dinner guests shouted, "Nasruddin! Your behavior is simply outrageous! Why are you grabbing at all the food and stuffing it into your mouth with your two hands like that?"

"Why?" repeated Nasruddin, his mouth full. "Because these two hands are all I've got!"

125. WHY PEOPLE YAWN

Nasruddin was staying at the house of relatives in a distant town. He had arrived in time for dinner, but so far they hadn't served him any food at all.

The evening was dragging on as his host regaled Nasruddin with stories in which Nasruddin had no interest.

Finally, Nasruddin could not help himself: he yawned.

This prompted his host to change the topic. "You are a learned man, Nasruddin," he said. "Why is it that people yawn?"

"It's either from lack of sleep or lack of food," declared Nasruddin. "And I got a very good night's sleep last night!"

126. THE MISER'S SOUP

A notorious miser had invited Nasruddin to dinner.

Nasruddin arrived at the appointed time and eagerly sat down at the dinner table.

"I have prepared soup, Nasruddin! I hope you will enjoy it," said his host as he placed two bowls of soup on the table.

Nasruddin stared for a moment at his bowl and then, without a word, he got up and started to undress.

"Nasruddin, what on earth are you doing?"

"I'm going to dive into the soup bowl and see if there might be a bit of vegetable or even some meat down there at the bottom."

127. NASRUDDIN'S BIG POT

Nasruddin brought some friends home. He seated them at the table and then went into the kitchen.

"But we have no food!" his wife said. "No meat, no rice, no vegetables, nothing. We don't even have wood to light a fire to cook with."

"I'll think of something," said Nasruddin.

He looked around the kitchen, grabbed their biggest cooking pot, and went into the other room.

"Dear friends," he said, "if we had any meat or rice or vegetables, or wood with which to light a fire, this is the pot I would use to cook a soup for you!"

128. NASRUDDIN AND THE DUCKS

Nasruddin was walking home from the bakery with some fresh bread, and then he saw them: ducks! Several very beautiful, very fat ducks were swimming in the pond by the side of the road.

Nasruddin ran at top speed into the pond, hoping to catch one of them, but the ducks all flew away.

Nasruddin then began to eat the bread, pulling off pieces and ostentatiously dipping each piece in the water before he ate it.

A man walking along the road shouted, "Hey, Nasruddin, what are you doing there in the pond?"

"I'm eating duck soup!" he replied happily.

129. NASRUDDIN AND THE RECIPE

Nasruddin's wife had written out the recipe for Nasruddin's favorite liver-and onion dish and then she sent him to the market.

"Buy all the ingredients," she said, "and make sure the liver is fresh."

Walking home, Nasruddin was daydreaming about the fine dinner he would enjoy when out of nowhere a crow swooped down and attacked him. As Nasruddin defended himself, the crow snatched the liver and flew away with it.

"You accursed creature!" Nasruddin shouted as the crow flew away. "But the joke's on you: you forgot the recipe. You don't have any idea how to prepare the dish!"

130. NASRUDDIN IS TIRED

"Go to the market and buy some meat for tonight's stew!" said Nasruddin's wife.

"I'm tired," he complained, but he went to the market.

Later on she said, "Bring in some firewood!"

"I'm tired," he groaned, but he brought in the firewood.

Next she told him, "Fetch some water!"

"Didn't you hear me say I was tired?" he moaned, but he brought the water.

"Come eat dinner!" she said.

"I can see there's no point in telling you how tired I am," Nasruddin sighed, and then he raced to the dinner table so fast he almost tripped over his robes.

131. NASRUDDIN'S VIEWS ON CHEESE

"Bring me some cheese," Nasruddin said to his wife. "Cheese is healthy, and it's tasty too. They say it's good for your bones. I like cheese very much."

"I don't think we have any cheese," Nasruddin's wife replied apologetically.

"Just as well I suppose," said Nasruddin. "They say cheese is hard on the stomach and it always gives me gas. I really don't like cheese at all."

"I don't understand," said Nasruddin's wife, now very confused. "Do you like cheese, or do you not like it?"

"That depends on whether there's any cheese in the house or not," replied Nasruddin.

132. NASRUDDIN EATS THE WALNUTS AND THE SHELLS

Nasruddin was eating some walnuts, shells and all.

"What on earth are you doing?" asked his wife, surprised. "Why don't you crack the shell and take the nut out before you eat them?"

"Well," said Nasruddin. "I already know there's a walnut in there, so I don't need to crack the shells in order to find that out."

He then ate another walnut in the shell.

"Plus, when I paid for these, I paid by the pound, shells and all. If I throw away the shells, that's like throwing away money!" Nasruddin explained. "This way, I'm getting my money's worth."

133. NASRUDDIN EATS AN APPLE

Nasruddin walked by the grocer's stall in the market. He was feeling very hungry, but he didn't have any money.

As he looked at the heap of apples on display, Nasruddin could not resist. He reached out, grabbed one of the apples, and bit into it. "Delicious!" he exclaimed.

"Hey there!" shouted the grocer. "You can't do that!"

"What do you mean?" asked Nasruddin.

"I mean you can't eat that apple without paying for it," shouted the grocer. "It's not ethical!"

"Oh, that's not a problem!" Nasruddin replied happily. "I'm eating this apple because it's nutritional, not because it's ethical."

134. WHERE'S THE HALVAH?

Nasruddin went to the grocer.

"I want some halvah, please," he said.

"My apologies," said the grocer. "I don't have any halvah."

"That's impossible!" exclaimed Nasruddin. "How can a grocer not have halvah? I simply don't understand. Tell me: do you have any flour?"

"Yes," said the grocer.

"And what about sugar? Do you have any sugar?"

"Yes," said the grocer.

"And do you have butter? Surely you have butter!"

"Yes," said the grocer.

"So, isn't it obvious? Everything you need is here!" Nasruddin concluded. "If you have flour and sugar and butter, why don't you go make some halvah?"

135. NASRUDDIN AND THE BOX

Nasruddin's friend gave him a box for safekeeping. "I'll be back to collect it tomorrow or the day after. But whatever you do, don't look in the box!"

"I understand," said Nasruddin. "Don't worry."

"Thank you!" said Nasruddin's friend, and he left.

Of course Nasruddin immediately opened the box. There was baklava inside!

He ate one piece.

Then another.

And another.

Finally he had eaten it all.

When his friend returned for the box, he opened it and saw it was empty.

"What happened to the baklava?" he asked.

"Don't ask," Nasruddin replied, "and I won't have to tell you."

136. NASRUDDIN AND THE BAKLAVA

Nasruddin was a holy man's disciple.

Another disciple brought their master a plate of baklava, and he didn't want Nasruddin to eat any.

"This is from our master's enemies," he told Nasruddin. "I suspect it's poisoned, so don't touch it!"

The disciple left, and Nasruddin couldn't resist. He grabbed the baklava, but he dropped the plate. Crash!

The other disciple rushed in to see what had happened and found Nasruddin down on all fours, eating baklava.

"I dropped the plate!" Nasruddin confessed. "In my shame, I wanted to die, so I'm eating as much of the poison as I can."

137. NASRUDDIN'S LUNCH

Nasruddin was working as a laborer, and each day he ate lunch in the company of his fellow workers.

"Nothing but bread and cheese," Nasruddin would say each day as he looked longingly at the food the other men had for their lunch. He saw dolmas, kebabs, tabbouleh, yogurt, pilaf, all kinds of food.

"You complain like this every day," one of the men said to Nasruddin. "You should tell your wife to make you something different for lunch."

"I'm not married," said Nasruddin.

"Who makes your lunch then?"

"I do," Nasruddin admitted, staring sadly at his bread and cheese.

138. NASRUDDIN DIVIDES THE WALNUTS

"Help us!" the boys said to Nasruddin. "We have this bag of walnuts but we don't know how to divide them."

"Do you want to divide them God's way, or the human way?"

"God's way!" shouted the boys.

So Nasruddin gave two handfuls to one boy, a handful to another, a few walnuts to the third, and none to the fourth.

The boys looked at him in confusion.

"All things come from God, not just walnuts," Nasruddin explained. "Life itself is a gift from God! As for walnuts: he gives more to some, less to others, and some get none."

139. WALNUTS AND WATERMELONS

One afternoon, Nasruddin was resting in the shade of a walnut tree next to a watermelon patch.

"What a strange world this is!" he exclaimed. "Tiny walnuts are growing on this enormous tree, while the watermelons are lying there in the dirt, growing on those scrawny vines. If I were in charge, I'd arrange things in a much more logical way."

Then a walnut happened to fall on Nasruddin's head.

"Praise God, now I understand!" he exclaimed. "It is because of Divine Providence that I was hit on the head by this tiny walnut and not by an enormous watermelon."

140. NASRUDDIN'S DEBT

Desperate for money, Nasruddin put his winter coat up for sale, and he soon found a buyer.

"Wait here," the buyer said, taking the coat. "I'll be right back with the money."

But the man did not come back, so Nasruddin lost his coat and still had no money.

As he walked past the baker's shop, he quietly grabbed some pastries which he took home for supper.

"O God," said Nasruddin, "I need you to please pay the baker for these pastries! You can just take it out of the money the man still owes me for my winter coat."

141. NASRUDDIN GETS A GIFT FROM GOD

Nasruddin was praying outside one night. "O God" he cried, "please reward me for my devoted service. I'm asking for a hundred gold coins, and I'll accept nothing less."

Nasruddin's neighbor heard this and, as a joke, he tossed down a bag containing some coins.

"Praise God!" Nasruddin exclaimed when he opened the bag and saw the money.

"Wait a minute!" shouted the neighbor. "You said you'd accept nothing less than a hundred gold coins. There's nowhere near that much in the bag."

"Since God kindly gave me this much now," Nasruddin shouted back, "he can owe me the rest."

142. NASRUDDIN NEEDS NEW CLOTHES

The whole town had put on their best clothes for the mayor's birthday parade.

Ashamed of his threadbare garments, Nasruddin was hiding in an alley as the parade went by. "O God," he prayed, "please give me some new clothes!"

At that moment, a man who had bought new clothes for the celebration threw his old clothes down into the alley. Joyfully, Nasruddin grabbed the bundle, only to discover these clothes were even more shabby than his own.

"God," said Nasruddin, "you're going to have to do better than this!" and he threw the bundle back up in the air.

143. THE DONKEY ON THE LEDGE

As Nasruddin was leading his donkey down a steep mountain path, the donkey stumbled and fell.

"O God," Nasruddin shouted, "if you save my poor donkey, I'll donate a gold coin to the mosque!"

Miraculously, the donkey landed on the ledge below. Nasruddin was amazed. "Thank you, God!" he exclaimed. "I had no idea you were so desperate for cash!"

Then the ledge under the donkey started to crumble.

"Okay, God, okay! I'll donate two gold coins."

Then the ledge collapsed and the donkey plunged to its death. Nasruddin sighed. "I never thought God would drive such a hard bargain."

144. THE COW AND THE COLT

Nasruddin's donkey had given birth but died in labor.

Nasruddin wanted to save the donkey's colt, but that meant giving it milk from the cow, and Nasruddin needed that cow's milk for his own family.

In despair, he prayed. "O God," he cried, "please relieve me of this burden and take the little colt into heaven as you did its mother."

Nasruddin was shocked to discover the next morning that his cow was dead, not the colt.

"O God," he cried, "I don't understand! How is it possible that you can't tell the difference between a cow and a donkey?"

145. BIG MOSQUE, LITTLE MOSQUE

Nasruddin had gone to the city to settle some business, but things were not turning out well.

"You should go pray in the big mosque," Nasruddin's business partner told him. "Maybe God will help us."

Nasruddin prayed in the big mosque, but his business still went badly.

He then went and prayed in a small mosque, and the next day he was able to settle his business matters favorably.

Nasruddin then returned to the big mosque and said, "Shame on you, big mosque! You look powerful and important, but it was the little mosque who finally helped me, not you."

146. NASRUDDIN AND GOD'S OWN GUEST

A dervish arrived at Nasruddin's house one night, dressed in fine garments and wearing an impressive turban. "I come as God's own guest," he proclaimed loudly, "and I thank you in advance for food and drink and also a bed in which to rest."

Without a word, Nasruddin took the dervish by the arm and led him down the street to the mosque.

"But this place is empty and cold!" shouted the dervish. "I will find no comforts here."

"You yourself said you were God's own guest!" replied Nasruddin. "So please make yourself at home here in God's own house."

147. THE DOOR TO NASRUDDIN'S HOUSE

Nasruddin had been robbed many times, but this was something new: a thief came in the night and stole Nasruddin's door.

When Nasruddin saw what had happened, he marched to the mosque and took that door off its hinges. He then carried it home and set it up in place of his own missing door.

"I recognize that door!" shouted his wife. "That's the door to the mosque. What do you think you're doing?"

"God only knows who stole our door," he replied. "And when God tells me the name of the thief, I'll return the door to his mosque."

148. NASRUDDIN AND HIS DOG

The imam came to see Nasruddin and discovered there was a dog in Nasruddin's kitchen.

"What is this unclean beast doing in your kitchen?" he shouted.

"This is my watchdog," said Nasruddin. "He's also good at herding goats."

"You must drive this dog out of your house before God sends his avenging angels to punish you!"

"About those angels," said Nasruddin, "are they going to watch out for thieves and herd my goats?"

"Of course not!" exclaimed the imam. "That's not a job for God's angels."

"Well then," said Nasruddin, "I think I'm going to have to keep my dog."

149. NASRUDDIN AND THE STRAY GOAT

A stray goat wandered into Nasruddin's yard. Nasruddin killed the goat and told his wife to cook the meat in a stew.

The goat stew was delicious, but then Nasruddin felt guilty about what he had done and confessed to his wife.

"You have committed a sin!" she shouted, shaking her fist at her husband. "God will call you to account."

"Then I'll tell God I never saw the goat," said Nasruddin.

"God might resurrect the goat as a witness!" his wife replied.

Nasruddin smiled and said, "Then I'll grab the goat and give it back to its real owner."

150. NASRUDDIN ON THE RUN

Nasruddin was making a journey through the mountains when he was attacked by a band of robbers. Thanks to some good luck he was able to escape, but he knew the robbers were not far behind him.

As he ran, he saw a wandering holy man beside the road. "Hide yourself!" Nasruddin shouted at the dervish. "Robbers are coming! They'll kill you for sure!"

"I serve God," replied the dervish, "and I know he will protect me."

"Well, that's good," said Nasruddin as he disappeared down the road. "But just in case, you might want to find a hiding place!"

151. NASRUDDIN AND THE SMALL BOAT

Nasruddin had gone fishing with a friend in a very small sailboat.

While they were far from shore, a sudden storm blew up unexpectedly. Fierce winds ripped the sails to shreds and waves tossed the boat back and forth.

When the little boat began to fill with water, Nasruddin was truly frightened. "What are we going to do?" he shouted at his friend.

"Do not worry," said his friend calmly. "Let us direct our prayers to God, who is great and merciful."

"God is great and merciful, I know," replied Nasruddin, "but this boat is small and it is sinking!"

152. NASRUDDIN AND THE SHIP'S PASSENGERS

Nasruddin was working on a ship, but he still made sure to say his daily prayers. The passengers all laughed at him, though, and they did not say their prayers.

Then, a sudden storm blew up and the ship was in danger of sinking. All the passengers began to pray loudly to God.

"O God," each passenger shouted, "you are great and merciful! Spare us! Please! I'll be a good Muslim! I'll dedicate my life to your service!"

After a while, Nasruddin shouted, "I see land ahead. We're saved!" And then he added, "You can stop your pretended devotions now."

153. NASRUDDIN'S HURRIED PRAYERS

Nasruddin was in a hurry when he went into the mosque to say his prayers.

When the imam saw how quickly Nasruddin was praying, he hit Nasruddin on the head. "Say your prayers again!" he commanded. "And show some respect this time."

Nasruddin said his prayers again, more slowly.

"That was better!" said the imam. "I'm sure God was more pleased with your prayers the second time than the first time."

"I'm not so sure," said Nasruddin. "The first time I said my prayers in obedience to God, but the second time I said my prayers in obedience to you."

154. NASRUDDIN NEEDS NEW SHOES

Nasruddin wasn't a wealthy man. His clothes were threadbare, and his shoes were even worse, much to Nasruddin's shame. He wanted to buy new shoes, but he couldn't even afford to pay the shoemaker to repair his old shoes.

A friend sought to console him. "Don't worry, Nasruddin," he said. "Your shoes may be shabby now, but God has promised that anyone suffering from need and want in this world will be rewarded in Paradise."

"I was thinking about that," replied Nasruddin, "and I realized there must be a lot of angels who are working as shoemakers there in Paradise."

155. NASRUDDIN'S INSHALLAH

"I'm going to buy a new donkey tomorrow," declared Nasruddin.

His wife rebuked him. "You should say 'Insh'allah!'"

But Nasruddin was feeling self-confident and refused to say "God-willing."

The next day he bought his donkey.

"I'm doing fine on my own!" he thought to himself.

But on the way home, a snake startled the donkey.

The donkey bolted, throwing Nasruddin into the brambles.

Nasruddin was scratched, his clothes were torn, and his donkey was gone.

It was dark when Nasruddin got home.

He knocked at the door.

"Who is it?" his wife asked.

"Nasruddin!" he replied. Then he added, "Insh'allah!"

156. WHO GETS THE LOAF OF BREAD?

Nasruddin was traveling together with an ascetic and a scholar, and they had found four loaves of bread.

They each ate one loaf, and then quarreled about the fourth.

Nobody wanted to share, so Nasruddin said, "Whoever has the best dream gets the bread!"

The next morning, the ascetic said, "I dreamed I kissed God's feet. What could top that?"

The scholar said, "My dream's better: God embraced me and praised my wisdom!"

Then Nasruddin said, "In my dream, God came to me and said, 'Nasruddin, what are you lying there for? Go eat the bread now!' So I did."

157. NASRUDDIN SEES AS GOD SEES

Nasruddin was preaching about the divine mysteries. "A thousand years on earth are but one second in God's time," he proclaimed. "Let us see as God sees in order that we may make a heaven on this earth."

"What a fine sermon!" said Nasruddin's neighbor afterwards. "I'm wondering if money works the same way as time. What do a thousand gold coins mean to you?"

"They mean less than a single copper coin!" Nasruddin replied.

"In that case, could you loan me a thousand gold coins?"

"Of course!" said Nasruddin. "Just wait a divine second while I go get them."

158. NASRUDDIN COMMANDS THE TREE

"I'm actually a saint," Nasruddin told his neighbor. "And as a saint, I have supernatural powers."

"Prove it!" said his neighbor. "If you have supernatural powers, command that tree over there to come here and bow down to you."

"O Tree," shouted Nasruddin, "come here and bow down to me!"

The tree did not move.

Nasruddin waited a moment, and then he walked over to the tree and bowed down before it.

"What are you doing?" asked his neighbor.

"Saints like me are also very modest," Nasruddin explained. "If the tree won't come to me, I'll go to the tree."

159. NASRUDDIN BY NIGHT

"You wouldn't know it just by looking at me," said Nasruddin, "but I have truly miraculous powers."

Nasruddin's friend laughed. "So tell me," he said, "what is your most miraculous power?"

"I can see in the dark! In the darkest darkness, I can see as clearly as if it were broad daylight. I need no light of any kind."

"Surely you're joking!" his friend objected. "I've seen you carrying a lantern in the dark, just like everybody else does."

"Of course!" said Nasruddin, smiling. "But I carry a lantern in the dark only so that others won't run into me."

160. NASRUDDIN'S TEARS

The imam of Nasruddin's village was delivering a sermon about the prophets, extolling their excellent qualities and illustrious deeds.

As the imam was speaking, Nasruddin began to weep loudly.

"Behold this man's sincere devotion!" the imam exclaimed. "My sermon has moved him to tears."

"It's true," said Nasruddin, sobbing. "This morning, I woke up to discover that my favorite goat had suddenly passed away, and it broke my heart. As I watch your beard wagging back and forth as you speak, it makes me think of my poor dead goat, and I can't help but weep these tears of sorrow."

161. NASRUDDIN'S LULLABY

Nasruddin's wife had just given birth, but the baby was restless. She rocked the baby, sang to him, doing everything she could to lull the infant to sleep, but nothing seemed to work.

"I'll take care of it," said Nasruddin.

"You don't know anything about babies!" his wife replied.

"But I know how to put people to sleep," said Nasruddin. "My pupils often fall asleep during my lectures. I'll try lecturing first, and if that doesn't work, I'll give him this boring book to read." Nasruddin took a book down off the shelf. "It puts me to sleep every time!"

162. THE TURBAN OF A SCHOLAR

People who could not read would sometimes bring letters to Nasruddin so that he could read the letters to them.

One man had brought Nasruddin a letter to read, but the handwriting was terrible.

"This is the worst handwriting I have ever seen," said Nasruddin. "I can't read this letter."

The man was indignant. "You wear the turban of a scholar, but you can't even read a simple letter from my brother."

Nasruddin pulled the turban off his head and threw it at the man. "Go ahead! Take the turban," he said, "and see if you can do any better!"

163. THE EAGLE JALIZ

A scholar was boasting about his knowledge of Islamic traditions. What color was Mohammad's horse? The scholar knew. What is the favorite food of the angels? He knew that too.

Eager to display his knowledge, Nasruddin shouted out, "Jaliz!"

The scholar stared at him coldly. "Is that some kind of name?"

"It's the name of the eagle who swooped down and carried Moses away," replied Nasruddin.

"But there is no record of an eagle swooping down and carrying Moses away."

"Well," retorted Nasruddin, "then Jaliz is the name of the eagle who did not swoop down and carry Moses away."

164. WHAT IS BREAD?

Some renowned wise men challenged Nasruddin to a contest. Nasruddin agreed, provided he could ask the first question.

This was his question: What is bread?

The wise men wrote their answers on pieces of paper. Nasruddin then read their answers aloud:

Bread is made with flour and water.

Bread is my favorite food.

Bread is a gift of God.

Bread is delicious.

Bread is baked in an oven.

Bread is the staff of life.

Nasruddin sighed. "These supposed wise men cannot even agree what bread is! Why then should we listen to what they say about matters of real difficulty?"

165. NASRUDDIN AND THE BUTTERFLY

Nasruddin was obsessed with butterflies. Whenever he saw a butterfly, he would stop whatever he was doing and watch the butterfly. He would get up and follow the butterfly, going wherever the butterfly would go until finally it would flutter away.

"I must learn what a butterfly truly is!" Nasruddin declared, so he got a net and caught a butterfly.

Then he took the butterfly and carefully removed its wings.

Next he removed the two antennae, and then the legs, and also the head.

"I can see all the butterfly's parts now," said Nasruddin. "But where did the butterfly go?"

166. NASRUDDIN PLAYS THE LUTE

"I can play any instrument!" Nasruddin declared confidently.

His friend gave him a lute. "Play this!" he said.

Nasruddin grabbed the lute and awkwardly strummed a single chord. He then strummed the same chord over and over, smiling contentedly the whole time.

"That sounds horrible," Nasruddin's friend protested. "Real lute players move their hands up and down when they are playing music on the lute."

"That's because they don't know what they're doing, unlike me," retorted Nasruddin. "They are unsure where to find the notes they are looking for, but I know exactly the chord that I want to play."

167. NASRUDDIN'S GRAMMAR

Nasruddin was traveling by ship, and a famous scholar was also on board.

Every time Nasruddin spoke, the scholar mocked him. "I've never heard such atrocious language. Didn't you study grammar in school?"

Nasruddin shook his head.

"Well," said the scholar, "I'd say you've wasted your life."

The ship was then caught in a storm.

"Abandon ship!" shouted the captain.

Nasruddin then turned to the scholar and asked, "Didn't you study swimming in school?"

The terrified scholar shook his head.

"Well," said Nasruddin, "I'd say you've wasted your life."

Nasruddin then jumped into the water and swam safely to shore.

168. NASRUDDIN'S SERMON

Nasruddin was preaching in a village for the first time.

"Do you know what I'm going to say?" Nasruddin asked.

"No!" the people shouted.

"How can I preach to people so ignorant?" he said and left.

They begged him to come back.

"Do you know what I'm going to say?" he asked again.

"Yes!" they shouted.

"Good! We can all leave."

But they asked him to try one more time.

"Do you know what I'm going to say?" he asked.

"Yes!" shouted some. "No!" shouted others.

"So let those who know teach those who don't!"

That was Nasruddin's last sermon.

169. THE CENTER OF THE UNIVERSE

There was a fortune-teller in the marketplace who resented Nasruddin boasting about how wise he was.

"If you're so wise," he said to Nasruddin, "please tell me: where is the center of the universe?" Then he added by way of emphasis, "The exact center."

Nasruddin stroked his beard, looking thoughtful. He then walked over to his donkey and stared at him intently.

"The exact center of the universe," Nasruddin declared, "is under my donkey's right hind hoof."

"Impossible!" retorted the fortune-teller. "You must prove to me that you're right!"

"No," said Nasruddin, "you must prove to me that I'm wrong."

170. THE SCHOLAR'S KNIFE

The governor issued a decree that nobody in the city was to carry any kind of weapon in public, including knives.

So, when Nasruddin was caught carrying a knife – and it was a very big knife! – they took him to court.

"Why were you carrying that knife?" asked the judge.

"I need it for my work," replied Nasruddin.

"What are you, some kind of butcher?"

"No, I'm not a butcher. I'm a scholar. I use the knife to scrape off errors in manuscripts."

"Why such a big knife?"

"You wouldn't believe the size of some of these errors, Your Honor!"

171. NASRUDDIN MEETS THE GOVERNOR

After a long journey, Nasruddin returned from the big city to his hometown. He looked like some kind of conquering hero, riding proudly on his donkey.

The people all gathered around. "Tell us about your visit to the big city, Nasruddin!" they said.

"Well," replied Nasruddin, as he grinned happily at everyone in the crowd, "the governor himself spoke to me!"

"Oooh!" said some people in the crowd. "Ahhhh!" said others.

"And what exactly did he say to you?" asked Nasruddin's wife.

"He said: 'Get out of my way, you idiot!' Those were the words the governor spoke to me."

172. THE GOVERNOR REWARDS NASRUDDIN

Nasruddin once did a favor for the governor, and the governor announced that he was going to bestow on Nasruddin a great reward. Naturally, Nasruddin was curious what reward the governor would give him.

"Nasruddin," said the governor, "because of your great service to me and to the state, I offer you my eternal friendship."

Nasruddin thought for a moment before he replied. "Thank you, Governor. That is very kind of you," he said. "But if you don't mind, I think I would rather you offered me some gold coins or perhaps a donkey. That would be far more useful."

173. THE GOVERNOR'S SURVEY

The newly appointed governor of the province summoned Nasruddin for an urgent consultation.

"I'm worried," said the governor, "and I need your advice. In my brief time here in the province, I've already met quite a few people who are undoubtedly insane. I find this troubling, and I think we need to conduct a survey to find out just how many people in the province are suffering from insanity. What do you think?"

"Well, Governor, I don't think that's the right approach," replied Nasruddin. "What makes you suspect there are any sane people here in the province to begin with?"

174. THE GOVERNOR'S POETRY

The governor considered himself a poet, and one day he asked Nasruddin to listen to his latest poem.

"The content is extremely tedious," Nasruddin told him afterwards, "and the style is even worse."

Enraged, the governor put Nasruddin in jail.

Time passed.

The governor had composed a new poem and decided to give Nasruddin a second chance. He summoned Nasruddin back to court, recited the new poem, and then asked his opinion.

Without a word, Nasruddin got up and started to leave the room.

"Just where do you think you are going?" shouted the governor.

"Back to jail," replied Nasruddin.

175. GUARDS AND THIEVES

Nasruddin was walking around the perimeter of the imperial palace one day, and he decided to speak with the palace guards standing along the wall.

"Greetings!" said Nasruddin.

The guards nodded silently in reply.

"I would like to know what your duties are exactly. Can you tell me why you are standing guard here?" asked Nasruddin.

"We stand guard to keep any thieves from climbing over the wall."

"I see," said Nasruddin. "And are you more concerned about thieves from outside who are trying to get into the palace, or thieves inside the palace who are trying to get out?"

176. EMPEROR TAMERLANE'S TAX COLLECTOR

Tamerlane was convinced that his tax collector had been cheating him. "Bring the tax collector here! And his account books too!" shouted the emperor.

When the tax collector arrived with his account books, Tamerlane interrogated him. Not satisfied with the answers, Tamerlane made him eat the books page by page.

"Nasruddin," Tamerlane shouted, "you are now my new tax collector."

When Tamerlane later summoned Nasruddin to bring the account books, Nasruddin wheeled in a cart full of bread.

"What on earth is that?" the emperor asked.

"I wrote the accounts on these loaves of bread," explained Nasruddin. "Just in case."

177. NASRUDDIN AND THE ROAST PHEASANT

“Ah, roast pheasant! My favorite!” said Emperor Tamerlane. “Nasruddin, you will carve and serve.”

“I offer you the head, O Head of the World,” he said to Tamerlane.

“The wings are for you,” he said to the Treasurer, “so you can fly off as soon as your embezzlement is discovered.”

“Here are the legs,” he said to the General, “for running from battle.”

“Take the neck,” he said to the Prime Minister, “for you’re sure to be hanged sooner or later.”

“The rest of the pheasant is mine,” Nasruddin concluded, “because I have done such an excellent job of carving.”

178. THE EMPEROR AND THE EGGPLANTS

Tamerlane had become obsessed with eggplants. He wanted to eat eggplants every day. "Aren't eggplants the best food in the world?" he asked Nasruddin.

"Yes, sire," said Nasruddin, "eggplants are the best."

Eventually the king got tired of eating eggplants. "Take this away!" he shouted. "I never want to see another eggplant."

Then he said to Nasruddin, "Aren't eggplants the worst food in the world?"

"Yes, sire," said Nasruddin, "eggplants are the worst."

"But didn't you tell me the other day that eggplants are the best?"

"Yes, sire," said Nasruddin. "My loyalty is to the emperor, not to the eggplants."

179. A GIFT FOR THE EMPEROR

Nasruddin was bringing a gift of coconuts to the emperor when another courtier stopped him.

"Give him apricots instead," he whispered to Nasruddin. "Ripe apricots. As ripe as possible. Trust me."

Nasruddin heeded the courtier's advice and returned with a tray of apricots.

"For you, O Great One!" said Nasruddin.

The emperor, however, was in a foul mood. "What kind of gift is this!" he shouted as he pelted Nasruddin with apricots.

"Thanks be to God!" shouted Nasruddin. "Thanks be to God!"

"Why are you thanking God like that?" Tamerlane asked.

"I'm thanking God those are apricots instead of coconuts."

180. TAMERLANE AND NASRUDDIN'S DONKEY

"My donkey is so smart I could teach him to read," declared Nasruddin.

The emperor laughed. "Teach him to read, and I'll give you a hundred gold coins."

Nasruddin hurried home, took a book, and put barley between the pages. The donkey turned the pages with his tongue, eating all the barley.

Over time, Nasruddin reduced the amount of barley between the pages. Then, he returned to Tamerlane.

"Behold: the donkey who reads!"

As the donkey turned the pages and didn't find any barley, he started to bray.

"That's not reading!" objected Tamerlane.

Nasruddin laughed. "That's how a donkey reads!"

181. NASRUDDIN'S BOLD CLAIM

When Nasruddin was a new minister in Tamerlane's court, he wanted to win the emperor's favor, so he made a bold claim.

"I have an announcement to make!" Nasruddin shouted. "I am actually God in human form."

"Prove it!" replied Tamerlane. "You can't expect us to accept such a claim without proof."

"I have supernatural powers," Nasruddin said calmly. "For example, I can read minds. As God, I can see into every heart and know what people are thinking."

"Then tell me what I'm thinking right now," said Tamerlane.

"Right now," Nasruddin replied, "you're thinking that I am a liar!"

182. NASRUDDIN THE PHILOSOPHER

A philosopher from a distant land came to Tamerlane's court. "I wish to challenge your philosopher!" he said.

"Nasruddin is my philosopher," replied Tamerlane, and he summoned Nasruddin.

"I will ask you a question," said the foreign philosopher.

"Ask me anything," replied Nasruddin.

"What is the number of stars in the sky?"

Nasruddin smiled. "That's an easy one! The number of stars in the sky is exactly equal to the number of the hairs in my donkey's tail."

"Absurd!" replied the foreign philosopher. "How can you prove it?"

"If you don't believe me," Nasruddin replied, "you can count them yourself."

183. NASRUDDIN'S QUALIFICATIONS

"You're going to be my new judge!" Tamerlane said to Nasruddin, but Nasruddin didn't want the job.

"O Emperor," Nasruddin said apologetically, "I'm not worthy of this honor."

"What do you mean you're not worthy?" exclaimed Tamerlane.

"Well, a judge must be worthy and also truthful," said Nasruddin, "isn't that correct?"

"Yes," said Tamerlane, "that's correct."

"As I already said: I'm not worthy. If I spoke the truth, that disqualifies me: I'm not worthy. If I'm lying and I really am worthy, then I'm disqualified because I'm a liar. Either way," Nasruddin concluded, "I'm not qualified to be your judge."

184. NASRUDDIN THE ARCHER

Tamerlane and his generals were boasting about their archery skills.

"I'm a rather skilled archer myself," proclaimed Nasruddin.

"Is that so?" said Tamerlane, laughing. "Come and show us!"

That was not what Nasruddin expected…

Tamerlane led them all to a field where targets had been set up. Nasruddin's first shot didn't even hit the target.

"I'm just showing you how my father used to shoot."

The next shot landed on the outside rim of the target.

"That's how my brother shoots," Nasruddin said.

On his third shot, Nasruddin hit the center. "And that," he exclaimed triumphantly, "is how I shoot!"

185. NASRUDDIN AND TAMERLANE'S WHIP

Serving in Tamerlane's court, Nasruddin saw the emperor engage in many acts of cruelty. Whenever possible, Nasruddin tried to intervene.

One time, the guards brought in a soldier. "He was passed out drunk while on duty, Your Highness," they said.

"I sentence him to five thousand lashes!" the emperor shouted.

Nasruddin burst out laughing.

"What's so funny?" asked Tamerlane.

"O Emperor," Nasruddin replied, "I was just thinking that either you've never been whipped, or perhaps you don't know how to count."

Tamerlane also started laughing and reduced the sentence to just fifty lashes.

Nasruddin's laughter thus saved the soldier's life.

186. NASRUDDIN AND THE KING'S GALLOWS

"No more lies!" shouted the king. "Henceforth, everyone tells the truth."

The king then built a gallows by the palace gate.

"Truthtellers shall pass through; liars will be hanged!" the king declared.

Nasruddin arrived at the gate.

"Where are you going?" asked the king.

"I'm going to be hanged."

"You are lying!" protested the king.

"Correct," said Nasruddin, "I was on my way to the barber. So hang me!"

Then he grinned. "But you can't hang me, can you? Because then I'd be telling the truth."

Thus Nasruddin persuaded the king to revoke his decree and take down the gallows.

187. NASRUDDIN AND THE KING'S ASTROLOGERS

"Tell me how long I will live!" the king shouted at his four royal astrologers.

"Five years!"

"Ten years!"

"A hundred years!"

"You will live forever!"

"These astrologers are all worthless," said the king. "Their numbers are too low or too high. Executioner, behead the four royal astrologers."

Then the king turned to Nasruddin. "Tell me what you think, Nasruddin: how long will I live?"

Nasruddin smiled. "An angel told me the answer to that question in a vision last night," he told the king. "Behold, said the angel, you and the king will die on the very same day!"

188. NASRUDDIN AND THE MAYOR'S FUNERAL

It was the day of the mayor's funeral. Nasruddin and the mayor had been enemies for many years, but Nasruddin's wife decided they were both going to the funeral.

"Let bygones be bygones," she said. "Hurry, or we'll be late!"

She was ready to go, but Nasruddin had not even started to get dressed yet.

"Nasruddin!" she yelled. "You have to get dressed! It's not polite to show up late to a funeral."

"I don't think I'm going to go to the mayor's funeral," Nasruddin replied. "What's the point after all? He is certainly not going to come to mine."

189. THE WEALTHY MAN'S FUNERAL

There was a funeral procession in the town for a very wealthy gentleman. Nasruddin put on his robes of mourning and joined in the procession, weeping copious tears and bewailing the deceased.

"Nasruddin," said one of his friends, "what are you doing here? I didn't even know that you were acquainted with this man. I'm surprised to find you here mourning his death with such feeling."

"I didn't know him," sobbed Nasruddin. "I never met him, not even once. Which is why I am certain that he has not remembered me in his will. That's the reason why I'm weeping!"

190. WATCHING A FUNERAL PROCESSION

Nasruddin and his young son were walking through the town when they saw a funeral procession coming down the street. The boy had never seen a funeral procession before.

"What is that?" he asked.

"That is a funeral procession," Nasruddin explained. "There is a dead person in the casket."

"And where are they taking the casket?" asked the boy.

"They are taking it to a place of darkness without food or drink, without silver or gold, without comfort, without hope…" replied Nasruddin mournfully.

"I don't understand," said the little boy. "Do you mean they are taking him to our house?"

191. NASRUDDIN'S FUNERAL ROBES

Nasruddin walked into the coffeehouse dressed as if he were going to a funeral. His friends, seeing his clothes, greeted him somberly and in hushed tones.

"My deep condolences," one of them said to Nasruddin. "Who is it that has died? I did not know there was a funeral today."

"Nobody has died," Nasruddin replied. "At least, not that I've heard. What makes you think someone has died?"

"You are wearing your funeral robes!"

"Oh, I see what you mean," said Nasruddin, looking down at his clothes. "I thought I should be prepared in case someone does die, that's all."

192. NASRUDDIN'S PET LAMB

Nasruddin had a beloved pet lamb, but his friends wanted to roast Nasruddin's lamb and eat it.

"Judgment Day is coming!" Nasruddin's friends told him. "We better eat that lamb of yours before the world ends."

Nasruddin agreed, and his friends organized a picnic.

While the lamb was roasting, everyone undressed and went swimming. Nasruddin, however, sat alone by the fire, and when the fire died down, he burned the clothes to keep the fire going.

Then his friends returned. "How could you burn our clothes?" they yelled.

"What's the difference?" Nasruddin replied. "You won't need clothes on Judgment Day."

193. NASRUDDIN'S FUNERAL ARRANGEMENTS

Nasruddin was getting his affairs in order because he had a sense that his life was coming to an end. He arranged his will, said goodbye to his friends, and then he gave strict instructions to his wife about his funeral arrangements.

"And the most important thing," he concluded, "is that you bury me in the ground upside-down: feet up and head down."

His wife was shocked. "That sounds very strange!"

"Everyone says that on the Day of Judgment, the whole world will be turned upside-down," Nasruddin explained. "When that happens, then I'll be the only one who is right-side-up!"

194. WHAT HAPPENS AFTER WE DIE?

As Nasruddin's fame as a wise man spread, people came from far and wide, seeking answers to life's big questions.

One day, a man came all the way from Baghdad to see Nasruddin. "I have a question for you," said the man. "I want to know what happens to us after we die."

Nasruddin paused for a moment, and then smiled.

"Come with me," he said. "I know who can answer your question."

Nasruddin then led the man through the streets of the city until they found themselves at the cemetery.

"You need to ask them," Nasruddin said, "not me."

195. PRAYERS FOR THE DYING

Nasruddin was summoned to the bedside of a dying man. The man had quite a bad reputation, but Nasruddin took pity on him and agreed to go.

"Pray for my soul to find peace in heaven!" he said to Nasruddin.

Nasruddin prayed, "May God help this poor man as he passes from this life."

Then he added, "May the Devil likewise help this poor man as he passes from this life."

"But I asked you to pray for my soul to find peace in heaven," the man protested.

"In your case," said Nasruddin, "we can't afford to take any chances."

196. NASRUDDIN'S WILL

Nasruddin went to see a lawyer about making a will.

"I'll be glad to help you," said the lawyer. "Just tell me how to divide your estate."

Nasruddin consulted a piece of paper he had brought with him. "A thousand gold coins to every member of my family, five thousand to the orphanage, another five thousand to the mosque, and then twenty thousand to distribute to the poor of the city."

The lawyer was amazed. "I had no idea you were so wealthy!"

"Oh, I don't actually have any money," Nasruddin explained. "But I still have great feelings of generosity!"

197. NASRUDDIN'S DEATH

Chopping wood in the forest, Nasruddin felt very cold. He'd never felt so cold! "I must be dead," he thought, so he lay down, stretched out like a corpse.

Then he realized his body had to be carried to the cemetery, so he went home to tell his wife. "I died in the forest. Tell my friends to come get my body."

Nasruddin returned to lie back down in the forest while his wife ran to the coffeehouse. "Nasruddin is lying dead in the forest," she sobbed.

"How do you know?" they asked.

"He came and told me," she replied.

198. NASRUDDIN IN THE CEMETERY

Taking a shortcut through the cemetery one night, Nasruddin fell into an open grave. He waited to see if angels would come greet him.

Then a loud noise frightened him, so he jumped out of the grave and ran.

The noise was a camel caravan, and Nasruddin's unexpected presence startled the camels. They bolted, spilling their cargo.

The camel-drivers, furious, beat Nasruddin badly.

"What happened to you?" asked Nasruddin's wife when he staggered home.

"I died and journeyed to the afterlife."

"Was it so bad there?"

"I think it would have been alright if I had not upset the camels."

199. NASRUDDIN ON HIS DEATHBED

Nasruddin's wife sat beside him on his deathbed, weeping uncontrollably.

"Don't cry, my dear," Nasruddin told her in a tremulous voice. "In fact, I want to see you wearing your best clothes and finest jewelry. And put on some makeup. It's very important that you look absolutely gorgeous."

"Oh, my dearest husband, I don't think I can do that," she replied sadly. "My grief is too great."

"Please, wife, just do what I say," Nasruddin insisted. "Then, when the Angel of Death arrives and sees you, he might change his mind and take you away with him instead of me!"

200. NASRUDDIN'S FINAL PRAYERS

The Angel of Death arrived to take Nasruddin. "It's time," said the Angel.

Nasruddin was alarmed. "I've done some dubious things in my life, and I haven't always been a good Muslim. Can you at least let me say the day's five prayers before I die?"

The Angel was compassionate and agreed. "I will be back tomorrow at this same time."

As promised, the Angel returned the next day.

"But I haven't finished my five prayers yet!" Nasruddin protested. "I've only done two."

"And when will you say the rest?" asked the angel.

"In my own time," Nasruddin replied, smiling.

STORY TITLE INDEX

34. Nasruddin and the Fish
35. How Old Is Nasruddin?
36. Nasruddin and the Stranger
37. Nasruddin in the Rose Garden
38. Nasruddin and the Eagle
39. Different People, Different Paths
40. Nasruddin's Buried Treasure
41. Nasruddin Is Perplexed
42. Nasruddin the Optimist
43. Nasruddin Digs a Hole
44. Nasruddin the Proud Father
45. Nasruddin in the Dark
46. Nasruddin's Sense of Economy
47. What the Quarrel Was About
48. Nasruddin's Lost Key
49. Nasruddin's Toothache
50. Nine Months for a Baby
51. Nasruddin's Wife and the Stew
52. How Old is Nasruddin's Wife?
53. No Room in the Bed
54. Itching and Scratching
55. Is Someone Snoring?
56. Spouses, Past and Present
57. The Sound of a Cloak
58. Nasruddin's Two Wives
59. Who Will Feed the Donkey?
60. The Burglar in the Well
61. The Bread in the Pond
62. Nasruddin Was Robbed
63. Nasruddin in the Cupboard
64. The Burglar in the Dark
65. Bags of Loot
66. The Thief with a Wagon
67. The Thief and Nasruddin's Rooster
68. Nasruddin and the Thief's Shoes
69. Nasruddin and the Apple Tree
70. Nasruddin and the Wind
71. Nasruddin the Nightingale
72. Nasruddin's Ladder
73. Nasruddin and the Tailor
74. Nasruddin and the Porter
75. Nasruddin and the Wealthy Merchant
76. Donkeys and Horses
77. The Cabbage and the Cooking-Pot

122. What a Beggar Needs
123. Honored Guests at the Banquet
124. Nasruddin's Two Hands
125. Why People Yawn
126. The Miser's Soup
127. Nasruddin's Big Pot
128. Nasruddin and the Ducks
129. Nasruddin and the Recipe
130. Nasruddin is Tired
131. Nasruddin's Views on Cheese
132. Nasruddin Eats the Walnuts and the Shells
133. Nasruddin Eats an Apple
134. Where's the Halvah?
135. Nasruddin and the Box
136. Nasruddin and the Baklava
137. Nasruddin's Lunch
138. Nasruddin Divides the Walnuts
139. Walnuts and Watermelons
140. Nasruddin's Debt
141. Nasruddin Gets a Gift from God
142. Nasruddin Needs New Clothes
143. The Donkey on the Ledge
144. The Cow and the Colt
145. Big Mosque, Little Mosque
146. Nasruddin and God's Own Guest
147. The Door to Nasruddin's House
148. Nasruddin and his Dog
149. Nasruddin and the Stray Goat
150. Nasruddin on the Run
151. Nasruddin and the Small Boat
152. Nasruddin and the Ship's Passengers
153. Nasruddin's Hurried Prayers
154. Nasruddin Needs New Shoes
155. Nasruddin's Inshallah
156. Who Gets the Loaf of Bread?
157. Nasruddin Sees as God Sees
158. Nasruddin Commands the Tree
159. Nasruddin by Night
160. Nasruddin's Tears
161. Nasruddin's Lullaby
162. The Turban of a Scholar
163. The Eagle Jaliz
164. What Is Bread?
165. Nasruddin and the Butterfly

STORY SOURCES

For story-specific bibliography and notes, visit:
Nasruddin.LauraGibbs.net

Birant, Mehmet Ali. Nasreddin Hodja: *The Turk Who Makes the World Laugh.*

Borrow, George. *The Turkish Jester.*

Downing, Charles. *Tales of the Hodja.*

Farzad, Houman (Diane Wilcox, translator). *Classic Tales of Mulla Nasreddin.*

Kabacali, Alpay. *Nasreddin Hodja.*

Mahfuzdur, Her Hakki. *202 Jokes of Nasreddin Hodja.*

Muallimoglu, Nejat. *The Wit and Wisdom of Nasraddin Hodja.*

Nakosteen, Mehdi. *Mulla's Donkey and Other Friends.*

Neruda, Nico. *The Little Book of Sufi Parables.*

Ohebsion, Rodney. *200+ Mullah Nasruddin Stories and Jokes.*

Rahman, Jamal. *Sacred Laughter of the Sufis.*

Sawhney, Clifford. *The Funniest Tales of Mullah Nasruddin.*

Shah, Idries. *The Exploits of the Incomparable Mulla Nasrudin.*

Shah, Idries. *The Pleasantries of the Incredible Mulla Nasrudin.*

Shah, Idries. *The Subtleties of the Inimitable Mulla Nasrudin.*

Shah, Idries. *The World of Nasrudin.*

Suresha, Ron. *The Uncommon Sense of the Immortal Mullah Nasruddin.*

Yorenc, Kemal. *The Best Anecdotes of Nasreddin Hoca.*

Printed in Great Britain
by Amazon